Justin—

RUTHLESS

Book 3 In the Jack Alexander Trilogy

*Thanks for buying the Book!
They tell me this might be my
Best work yet.
Happy Reading !!!
Enjoy
John*

By John Wendell Adams

May 2022

AMS Strategic Solutions Corporation
7548 North Crawford Avenue, Unit D
Skokie, IL 60076
Copyright © 2021 by John Wendell Adams

Visit our website at www.johnwendelladams.com
Published in Skokie, IL. AMS Strategic Solutions Corporation

Printed in the United States

First Edition July 2022

ISBN: 978-0-9903650-5-1 (soft copy)
ISBN: 978-0-9903650-1-3 (eBook)

10 9 8 7 6 5 4 3 2 1

Books may be purchased by contacting the publisher and author at the above address or by visiting www.johnwendelladams.com. Quantity sales: special discounts are available on quantity purchases by corporations, associations, libraries, and others. For details, contact the publisher at the address above.

Orders by U.S. trade bookstores and wholesalers: Please contact the publisher at the above address or visit www.johnwendelladams.com

Book Editing by Mary Harris
Cover Design by Monika Suteski
Book Trailer by Velocity Video Pro
Book Trailer Voice Over by Zach Zeidman

Thank you for buying Ruthless. Enjoy it!!!

PLEASE GIVE A REVIEW OF THE BOOK ON AMAZON

- Go to www.johnwendelladams.com
- From the home page, click on the Amazon icon
- Scroll down to "Customer Reviews"
- Move your cursor over the "5 stars"
- Choose and click on the one you want
- Here is where you can write your review

Thank you so much – John Wendell Adams

To the memory of my mother, Hazel Vivian Halliburton, who always believed in me, never gave up on me, encouraged me to strive to be the best, and most importantly, gave me life.

To the memory of my sister, Judi, who encouraged me the first time she heard I was going to write a novel. Every conversation with her was filled with inspiring words and new ideas.

To the memory of my best and life-long friend (and the brother I never had), Willie (Billy) Robertson, who always applauded my efforts and let me know I could achieve whatever I set my mind to.

I am doing a great work and I cannot come down.

Nehemiah 6:3 *New American Standard Bible NASB*

PROLOGUE

"Surprise!"

"Happy birthday, Clarence!" "Hey…we gotcha."

"I thought you said you couldn't be surprised."

"It took a while, but we pulled it off."

FBI SPECIAL AGENT HARPER HAD been startled. He was more shocked than surprised. He didn't think anyone outside of Human Resources knew his birth date. It hadn't come up and he certainly hadn't advertised it. Whenever the subject of birthdays came up, he had conveniently changed the subject. It wasn't so much he didn't want to acknowledge his birthday with his coworkers, he thought it was more appropriate with his wife and kids.

He speculated that it had been a bit strange and unusual when his boss told him he needed to show up at a meeting regarding new FBI mandates. It was strange because there hadn't been a general email announcing this. When he told his supervisor he had requested the day off a month ago, his boss replied, "Look, I'm under a lot of pressure to cover these changes for all of my direct reports. The meeting is scheduled for two and a half hours. The important stuff will last an hour, then you can leave."

Clarence still thought it was a little fishy until he saw the email from his boss to all the attendees. What he didn't know was everybody else received another communique to arrive thirty minutes earlier for Clarence's surprise birthday party.

When he walked into the big conference room ten minutes before the start of the supposed meeting, people were milling around, some were sitting down, others were talking among themselves, and nothing seemed out of the ordinary. As soon as he sat down, they all yelled in unison, "Surprise." He was so shocked, he bolted out of his seat.

Now his other colleagues and friends in the Bureau came in, walked over to him, and wished him happy birthday. On command, someone wheeled in a big cake and people started handing him wrapped presents. He was overwhelmed; his eyes started to fill with tears, he looked down, and the tears fell on his shirt. Someone got the attention of everyone and one by one, people started sharing comments about what a great guy, boss, colleague, or friend he was. Somebody else handed him a piece of cake and a fork. In some ways it felt to him like a wedding, as gifts started to mount up on a big side table and he saw this enormous double decker cake.

Little by little, he started to relax. He smiled, his shoulders slumped, and his eyes crinkled at the corners as he acknowledged the people who slapped him on the back and said, "Happy Birthday."

After thirty minutes passed, his boss raised his hands and asked people to quiet down. He then said, "I've got a few things to say. First, everyone in this room, in the department, and probably in the entire Bureau knows Clarence absolutely hates celebrating birthdays, and especially surprise birthdays. To be Anglo-Saxon and not celebrate birthdays is an oxymoron. I don't understand it because every other person in Clarence's family thrives on parties, especially birthday parties."

Everyone in the room started laughing and someone said, "Well, Clarence, we gotcha, we gotcha good!"

There was laughter all over again. His boss raised his hands again and said, "Okay, quiet down. Clarence, you have been a tremendous asset to this department and to the Bureau. Everyone in this room has the highest regard for you. The least we could do was surprise you with this party. We hope you have a great celebration with your family or whatever you decide to do. Just know, you are a part of our family. Again, happy birthday."

There was a round of applause. Clarence lifted his hands to get the group to calm down. He stepped forward and said, "Thank you all for this party. The chief is right, I didn't want this at all. You have been very kind with this cake, all these gifts, and your well wishes. I'm going to need to recruit a few of you to help drive all of these presents home with me "Laughter". But seriously, I am honored by your thoughtfulness and generosity. I will long remember this day. Thank you again." Applause.

Just as he finished, he noticed three men enter the room. One of them whispered something in the ear of Clarence's boss. The two conferred for a couple of minutes. Then the three men with his boss walked over to him. Their eyes were fixed on him, not veering to the left or the right. The three men camped themselves around him, so he had nowhere to go. The man who spoke to his boss said, "Agent Harper, I'm afraid I have to ask you to follow us to the Inspection Division's Internal Investigations Section."

He was surprised at both the message and the direct way he spoke. It was clear this was official business. Nonetheless, he asked, "What?"

The primary agent said, "All will be explained to you when we get to Internal Investigations. We need to leave here now. Let's go."

He looked over at Harry Coombs, his chief and asked, "Boss, what's up?"

"You tell me."

His facial expression turned hard and brooding like clouds darkening before a storm. Seeing this, his boss said, "Don't get all spun up about this until you know the details."

Clarence's face softened and he gave his boss a half smile. Then he said, "Hey…it must be another birthday party."

He turned toward the three men and said, "Okay, let's do this."

As the four men walked out of the room, every eye was fixed on them. While no one said anything, the unspoken words were, *this can't be good.*

CHAPTER

ONE

THE EXECUTIVE SESSION HAD BEEN spirited. The board of directors listened intently to Lenard Shapiro's report. As the current President and CEO of Universal Systems, he had invested many years of his life successfully advancing the interest of the company. When he first arrived at Universal, the press made a big deal of the fact he was the first Jewish CEO in the company's history. While there were many good, even great, things Lenard and his team had achieved over the last fiscal year, the board was disenchanted with year-over-year profits and the current stock price. Lenard was smart not to defend these two elements the board highlighted. His presentation focused on the strong areas, top line revenue growth, specific divisional gains, the introduction of new products and services, expansion into new markets, including China, and especially their recently acquired consulting division, JPC Consulting. It had been the company's "Star" and the industry was in awe of what it continued to achieve. The media regularly featured the division for its innovative approach and customer loyalty. Since Universal Systems was a publicly traded company, their financials reported on the conditions of all their divisions, including JPC. With all the excitement going on in the division, Lenard made sure to make JPC the last presentation over the two-day board meeting. He also made certain Jack Alexander, the president of the division, gave the board presentation.

The board agreed with Lenard. They, too, were interested in hearing the divisional update from Jack. Even before the acquisition of JPC Consulting four years ago, they were impressed with him. Of the people on Lenard's leadership team, the board was in awe of Jack. From his initial arrival at Universal, he excelled in every area of responsibility. Several of the board members considered him heir apparent for the role of President and CEO. Each presentation he made to them only increased his value proposition.

There had been a real concern as to whether he had fully recovered from the kidnapping incident three years ago. Back then, when he was made President of the newly acquired consulting firm, the CFO was jealous. She thought she should have been given the job. As a result, she took out a contract on Jack's life. Had it not been for the amazing work by the FBI, especially his good friend Special Agent Clarence Harper, and the Chicago police, her scheme might have succeeded.

It took him time to recover from the trauma of what happened. So, the board remained interested in seeing how he would recapture his zeal and business acumen. From every indication, he had. His year-over-year accomplishments were phenomenal. It was no secret he was being heavily recruited to be CEO at other firms. It was also no mystery he had the highest loyalty to Lenard. He regarded him as a father figure and a mentor. Lenard had groomed him in business and the ways of Universal Systems, almost from the day he'd hired him to work on his leadership team. He told Jack three things: '"I will fire you on the spot if you ever try to conceal anything company-related from me. You will always know where you stand with me. You should never repeat anything I tell you in confidence." Jack had agreed and had operated by them ever since.

Another aspect of significance for the board was Jack's ties to Chicago. They knew he was born and raised in the city. While he went off to college, he returned to marry and take up roots. In addition, his mother had a very successful business while he was growing up. Her bridal rental agency in downtown Chicago was an industry leader for almost 30 years. *Vivienne's Designs* thrived with a host of local celebrities, Miss Illinois, and Miss America contestants. His mother had the distinction of having a regular TV program on WBKB, a local television station. Jack saw entrepreneurial success up close.

Nonetheless, with all the great achievements of Jack and JPC Consulting, the board was not happy with the overall annual performance of Universal Systems.

"Lenard, we have shared with you our overall assessment of the firm's performance for the year. What we will need to see at our next board meeting is your plan to get the company back on track. As you are aware, we all have a responsibility to our shareholders. So, we need a plan to achieve the needed results."

Lenard made sure he didn't try to defend. He said, "We are on it! Trust me, each member of my leadership team is working hard on our recovery plan."

There were a few nods from the sixteen board members. They were a supportive group. Nevertheless, they needed to see the required course correction. After the last presentation, the meeting was adjourned. He made sure he spoke to and shook hands with each member before they left the conference room.

Shane McCarthy, the board chairman, cornered Len and asked to meet for a few minutes in Len's office. As soon as they sat down, Shane said, "Len, I have great faith in you and your abilities. Since I have been on the board, you have been a strong leader and the Chief Executive Universal has needed."

Len listened and tried not to show any facial expressions other than a smile. Instead of focusing on Shane's face or his mouth, he tried visualizing a happy memory. His forced his eyes to reflect a relaxed, warm state. It helped him keep from being defense.

Shane continued, "However, I've been hearing some grumblings from some of the board members. Having a down year hasn't helped. I've been told if the new plan for this upcoming fiscal year isn't compelling, some may be looking for a change in leadership at the top."

Len could tell Shane was sending him an uncomfortable message. Having observed Shane's behavior over the years, Len could tell whenever he was stressed because Shane's Irish face would turn beet red. His last comments simply hung in the air. He sat there, looked calmly at Shane, and waited to see if he had anything to add. Then he said with a half-smile, "Should I be packing my bags and clearing out my desk today."

"What?"

"I don't want to wait until the other shoe drops."

Shane had a pained expression on his face. He replied, "No one is ready to kick you out into the street."

"Hey, I get it. I've got to run to another meeting. Thanks for sharing."

Len was the first one to stand up. He extended his hand and briefly waited until Shane stood, reach out, and shook Len's hand.

****

Millennium Park, a massive place along Lake Michigan. The mayor of the city had spent millions investing in it. With different musical venues, a very nice restaurant, biking and running trails, it was a perfect place to walk and talk. Len had picked a bright, sunny day to spend time discussing the current dilemma with Jack.

"So, Len, what would you like me to do?"

Len and Jack had spent over an hour debriefing the board meeting. Len used most of the time sharing his overall reaction. "Look, based on all I heard today, I need to start looking for new employment."

"What?"

"Yeah, the old saying is, 'What have you done for me lately?'"

"Uh huh, but our new plan will be great. We're all working on our individual parts. Personally, my divisional plan is to double revenue for JPC and make it sixty percent more profitable than last year. That's my commitment to you and to Universal. So, trust me, the intent is to have all the corporate details assembled by the end of next week."

"Yeah, but do you know any really good headhunters?"

"Len, that's crazy talk."

"Fine, let me see what you folks come up with."

CHAPTER

TWO

THE DRIVE TO HIS CABIN in Wisconsin was one Len had made so many times he could almost do it in his sleep. He was looking forward to a nice, quiet getaway weekend with his wife, Ilana, who had gone up 3 days before. Nevertheless, as he drove, he was lost in his thoughts. *"However, I'm hearing some rumblings from some of the board members. If the new plan for this fiscal year isn't compelling, some may be looking for a change of leadership at the top..." Are they serious? They should be kissing my feet and laying down palm branches. A change in leadership...really? That's insane. I know Jack and Edmond won't let me down. They promised to ensure the new fiscal plan would be a winner. I've learned to count on them. We'll sort it out."*

Preoccupied, Len missed a turn on the road. When he tried to compensate for it by pumping the brakes, they didn't hold, and his car went off the side of the highway into a ravine. While it wasn't very deep, the car went up in the air. Because of the car's momentum, it crashed through the trees and tumbled almost to the ground and landed on the driver's side. Len lost consciousness after the car hit the uneven terrain.

When he came to, he had no idea how long he had been out. Nonetheless, he realized he was pinned in and could not get out of the car. He felt blessed when he realized his cell phone was in the inside pocket of his jacket. He struggled to pull it out but once he did, he couldn't get a signal. Then he remembered he was in a section of the road where cell towers were limited. He tried blowing his car's horn. But he wasn't sure if anyone would hear him. He tried to assess his physical condition. He felt a sharp pain in his right leg and an acute ache on the right side of his forehead. He looked down at his cell phone and saw one bar. He hit the speed dial to his wife's phone. It took forever to start ringing. Finally, it rang, and she answered,

"Len, where are you? You should have been here three hours ago. Are you all right?"

"Babe, call an ambulance and the highway patrol."

"What…oh my God! Where are you?"

"I hurt really bad. I'm not sure how long I can hold on."

"Which road are you on?"

"GPS!"

"Len, keep talking."

****

"Your husband is going to be fine. But he is fortunate to be alive. His car was suspended on a big tree. If the tree had given way, the car would have crashed at the bottom of a deep ravine. He has a broken right leg, a broken right arm, three broken ribs, and suffered a concussion. He will need to be in the hospital for an undetermined period."

****

Four days had passed before Jack was able to see Len. Jack sat in a chair next to Len's bed. As a precautionary measure, the doctors had Len hooked up to several devices so they could monitor his vital signs. Jack had immediately noticed the casts on both his leg and his arm. The leg cast extended above Len's knee and his leg was hoisted in the air above his head. The doctors had told him he would be laid up for an extended period. One of their main concerns was the concussion. Their tests had not revealed the full extent of the trauma to his head. So, they wanted to be extra careful.

Jack asked, "Len, how are you feeling and what happened?"

"A color TV, hospital food, and a call button... I'm on top of the world. I wish I knew."

"So, what happened exactly?"

"I wonder if the highway patrol has CCTV cameras. To see what happened would be helpful to us both."

"Len, are you saying there was something wrong with your car that caused the accident?"

"Maybe...your guess is as good as mine."

"Len, that's scary stuff. Do you think your car was unstable or had been tampered with?"

He watched Len as he considered the question. Then Len answered, "Tampered with? Who would do such a thing?"

Jack rubbed his chin, reflecting on Len's question. "I can get it checked out for you. I know a guy, a friend, who would do it as a favor to me."

He watched as Len pondered his offer. His eyebrows were slightly raised, and he didn't blink. After a few seconds, he said, "Might be a big waste of time."

"We need to check it out. In the meantime, rest up and get well. We need you back as soon as possible."

"What's up with the new fiscal year plan?"

"Len, are you kidding me? Two words…Rock solid"

Jack noticed Len's expression changing. He could always tell when Len had something difficult to say. He would look away and stare off into space. His hands would be folded. These were two telltale signs. So, he asked, "What's wrong? Is it something I said?"

Jack tried to see where Len's gaze went. Out of the window, a hospital attendant pushed a man in a wheelchair. They weren't in a hurry and the man was not looking at his surroundings; his focus was straight ahead. He looked back at Len and heard him say, "You have a presentation, but you don't have a presenter."

"What? You're the Man!"

"We need to put our best foot forward…this is what I believe. I'm not healthy enough to do it and I don't think I will be able to absorb it all by the board meeting."

Jack was shocked. He wasn't prepared for Len's comment. He said, "What? The presentation has your name all over it."

"The risk greatly outweighs the potential reward. You need to do it."

This time it was Jack who got quiet. He looked at Len, looked around the hospital room, and then down at his hands. As he did, he realized what Len had said was true. If the board presentation was not rock solid, it would have negative implications for the entire leadership team, especially for Len. Finally, he looked at Len and said, "Fine. But you'll need to send a note indicating I am only the stand-in for the pitch to the board with your approval."

"Okay…and the stand-in as CEO until I fully recover."

Jack would have fallen if he hadn't been sitting. He couldn't believe what Len had just said. "What? No…I'm not you and I already have a job as president of JPC."

"Great capacity is a strength of yours. You can do this, and much more. Trust me."

Jack was speechless. Len's trust in him was unwavering. Somewhere inside himself, he again realized Len was right. Yet, it was hard for him to embrace his suggestion. After additional reflection he reluctantly said, "Fine…but only until you're well enough to step back in."

CHAPTER
THREE

THE THREE MEN LED CLARENCE to the office of the director of the FBI Inspection Division's Internal Investigations Section (IDII). While it wasn't far from the room where his party was held, the three men walked in tight formation as if they were ensuring he didn't try to flee. He could think of no-good reason for him to be led away. Yet, he knew running away was not the answer. He tried engaging in a conversation with the leader of the trio, the guy who had talked to his boss.

"How long have you been in the Bureau?"

Clarence got no answer.

"What's the purpose of taking me to the Internal Investigations Section? I should at least know why."

Finally, he got a response,

"You probably are entitled to know. But I was only instructed to find you and escort you to the Director's office. If I knew more, I might share it with you, but I don't."

With those remarks, he was silent the rest of the way. It was unnerving for Clarence. As he walked along with his escorts, he wracked his brain to try and think of what he had done.

CHAPTER

FOUR

CLARENCE AND JACK HAD BEEN buddies in college. They'd met freshmen year. It turned out they met because of being in the same dorm room. Jack ran track and Clarence continued to excel on the football field. Since he had played both tight end and defensive linebacker, he decided to choose linebacker because he liked catching and tackling the opposition. He majored in political science while Jack majored in business administration. The two of them hung out together all the time. In fact, it was Jack who introduced him to Julie, the woman he would eventually marry. Jack was best man at his wedding, and later Clarence asked him to be godfather to his first son. When he considered working for the Bureau, he sought Jack's advice.

"For some reason I feel drawn to the FBI."

"Really?"

"Well, it's funny, I like the law, but I don't want to be a lawyer. I want to work for the government, but not as a politician. Law enforcement interest me, but I don't want to be a policeman. Once I get a law degree, I think the FBI will be a good fit for me."

"Hey, it's your choice."

"After my internship in Washington, DC and listening to so many stories about life overseas, I ruled out the CIA. The Secret Service is almost impossible to get into and I'm not sure I want to spend my life protecting the President."

"What does wifey say about it?

"No help there. She wants me to be safe and come home every night."

"So, decision made."

"No so fast. There is a battery of tests and some psychological exams. In the end, very few pass, and even fewer are chosen."

"Nothing ventured, nothing gained. The worst that could happen is you bomb, come home, get a job where I'm working, and see your bride every night."

He did go for it. Not only did he pass, but he earned one of the highest collective scores of anyone who ever applied to join the FBI. It was hard and brutal, but he pushed forward. Once he became an agent, he moved quickly through the ranks. For him, getting promoted was a regular occurrence.

When Jack came to him and asked for his assistance regarding Catherine Frazier bilking the Department of Defense, he was only too happy to help. By then, he was responsible for the Midwest District and was in Chicago. All during his time with the Bureau, he had been recognized for exemplary behavior. So, it was a total surprise to be sitting in the waiting room outside of the office of the Director for the Inspection Division's Internal Investigations Section.

He kept thinking, *"what in the world have I done that would require three armed escorts to bring me to this office?"* He began to reflect on his case files, trying to determine something he'd done wrong. After a protracted period in deep thought, he couldn't come up with anything. Then he realized he was supposed to be home by now. He took out his phone to call his wife. As he hit the speed dial, the leader of the escort trio told him, "Sir, please hang up right now. You are not allowed to make any phone calls. In fact, I am required to confiscate your phone."

"What?"

The agent reached out his hand. "Sir, please hand it over to me."

Clarence handed the agent his phone as instructed. At that moment, the door to the director's office opened and Evelyn Hammer walked out. They had never met. She had held training sessions he had attended. She was a tall woman, about five feet nine, late thirties. Her brown hair was cut so it stopped at her shoulders. Her eyes were an unusual shade of green. A colleague once told Clarence her eyes reflected her personality, somewhat relational but with a jealous streak. He still remembered the way she looked during one of her training sessions when someone asked her a question. Her eyes seemed to burn right through the guy as she listened to his question. But then she gave a sensitive response to the question. It was rumored she had joined the Bureau right out of law school. She was mentored and rose quickly through the ranks. The word was the IIS was simply a grooming spot for her.

She walked over to Clarence, looking him in the eye the entire time. As she approached, he stood. She was the first to speak. "Agent Harper, I'm Evelyn Hammer, Director of the Inspection Division's Internal Investigations Section. So nice of you to come visit me."

The sarcasm was obvious, but Clarence spoke his mind. "Why am I here? What is it you want from me?"

Director Hammer looked long and hard at him before she answered. "Agent Harper, glad you asked. Step into my office."

She moved aside and allowed him to walk in ahead of her. As he did, she whispered to the agents who brought him. "Stay here in case there is an incident."

She turned, walked in behind him, and closed the door. "Have a seat, Agent Harper. Pick any chair, except mine, of course."

He hesitantly sat down in one of the two chairs right in front of the Director's oversize desk. He watched her as she took her time walking around its side. He kept his eyes locked on her and she did the same. He waited as she finally sat down and picked up a file on her desk. He realized she was trying to get him off balance by slowly reviewing it as if for the first time. She read something in the file and then look at Clarence without saying a word. She did this for a protracted period. Finally, she spoke. "So, you are wondering why you are here?"

"Really?"

"And you can't think of any reason why you might be in this office?"

"Is this some kind of joke?"

"So, it would surprise you to know someone filed a complaint against you?"

Clarence thought for a few seconds and then said, "You are full of jokes today."

He was now perturbed. He didn't like the interrogation tactics she was using. Rather than come out with the details, she chose to string him along. Finally, she said, "It's a sexual harassment charge."

"Sexual harassment, huh? Who? When and where was this supposed to have happened?"

"You should tell me. I'd be interested in your account."

Clarence was incensed. "Is this a game you are playing? I don't think this is funny at all."

He continued to observe her every move. She had a deadpan expression, trying to conceal any emotions. Her eyes were closely focused on him as if she were trying to detect some telltale guilt signal. Then she said, "Why don't you come clean? Why make this more difficult than it needs to be?

At that point, he stood up. "Look, I've had just about enough of your empty threats and innuendos. Either tell me specifically what this is all about or I am leaving. I've had a perfect service record with the Bureau, and I don't deserve this kind of treatment."

"Okay, okay, Agent Harper. Please sit down."

Clarence stood his ground.

"Please, have a seat and I'll fill you in on all the details of the charge."

Slowly, he sat back down. He had one eyebrow positioned above the other. His lips were pressed so tightly together they were on the verge of splitting.

He watched as Director Hammer re-opened the file on her desk. She then said, "Agent Harper, do you know who Agent Carla Landers is? And was she one of the agents under your command?"

"Here we go again. One more attempt at humor and I am out of here." Clarence again noticed that the Director never took her eyes off him. He could tell she was looking for some indication of him trying to conceal something. He never blinked or looked away.

"Agent Harper, what was your relationship with her?"

"My relationship? You obviously must be bored with your job. You already know the answer to the question. What's the complaint?"

"She says you asked her to come to your hotel room when you and some members of your team were working on a case."

He watched as Hammer looked down at her notes. He interrupted her next comments by asking, "So, what was I was supposed to have done when she came to my hotel room?"

"Offered her a drink, asked her to sit down on the bed, and then started telling her how capable and attractive she was."

"You are kidding me right now?"

"You suggested she stay with you and relax for the rest of the night."

Clarence kept his cool. His face showed no emotion. He needed to get to the bottom of this. He knew from his years of interrogating criminals it was critical to remain calm. If he had any chance of getting the total story from Hammer about what was obviously a lie, he would need to quiz her without her totally realizing it.

"Are you reading from some lurid crime novel?"

"You asked her to go into the bathroom and put on some lingerie you'd provided. But she wouldn't do what you asked."

"This just keeps getting more ridiculous."

"You got up from where you were sitting, approached her, and tried to embrace her sexually. She rebuffed your attempts and walked out of your room."

He was so angry he was about to explode. But he calmed himself. His next question was asked so softly Hammer had to lean close to him to hear what he said. "This is what I'm being charged with?"

"Yes, and it would likely go better for you if you simply confessed now instead of this going before a committee where there would be a hearing. If you are convicted, it will both negatively and permanently affect your career with the Bureau."

He was steaming inside. He thought, *"this is obviously an attempt on someone's part to discredit me. Why, I do not know. Agent Landers knows fully well I never asked her to come to my hotel room at any time. In fact, in all my years with the Bureau, I have never had anyone, male or female, in a hotel room I've occupied. I'm glad I took my wife's advice to establish a practice of meeting everyone in a public place. In fact, whenever I checked into a hotel, I would have another agent go into my room first to insure there was no one in the room attempting to set me up. There are scores of agents who would testify to this. So, what's going on here? I don't, know, but I need to get to the bottom of this, one way or another."* Clarence asked, "Confessing…no way."

Clarence watched as Hammer tried to maintain her composure, but she squinted her eyes, and she was gritting her teeth. He felt like she might have spit in his face if she could have gotten away with it. But she maintained her self-control and said, "If you aren't going to confess right now, there will be a hearing in about three weeks. My advice to you, don't try anything like leaving the country."

"Not a chance."

They both exchanged irritating stares at each other before Hammer spit out, "You're free to go. Pick up any of your belonging from my assistant on your way out."

Clarence slowly got up, still staring at Hammer. He moved to the door. When he placed his hand on the doorknob, he turned around and said, "My wife, my family, and my career are too important for me to do something so stupid. If I were you, I'd be trying to figure out the motive for Agent Landers to make such a baseless claim."

With that comment, he turned, slowly opened the door, and strolled away without closing it. He walked up to the Director's assistant and asked, "Now that I am finished with your boss, please give me my phone."

CHAPTER

FIVE

THE BOARD OF DIRECTORS WASTED no time in calling a press conference. Once everyone was assembled in Universal's large conference room, Shane McCarthy, the board chairman, stood behind the lectern, cleared his throat, and called the meeting to order.

"Most of you are wondering why we called this press conference. Well, we have a few announcements to make. First, our President and CEO, Lenard Shapiro, was in a car accident. While he's very much alive, he has suffered some serious injuries that disallow him from continuing with his responsibilities. We are not yet certain how long he will be in the recovery process. We wish him God's speed for full and complete recovery. Second, during this temporary period, we have decided to make Jack Alexander interim President and CEO. He is the best person to fill this role as he is well respected both in Universal and in the industry. Most of you are aware of the superior job he has been doing as President of our JPC consulting division. He has taken the operation to heights we thought wouldn't happen for years to come. So, Jack will assume all of Len's responsibilities. Our confidence rests with the fact he has worked with Lenard directly for years. Lastly, he will continue to maintain the responsibilities for JPC consulting as well. We strongly believe he has the capacity to handle both roles until we know more about Lenard's ability to return."

Jack watched Shane McCarthy take a breath, looked around the room, and then down at his notes. Then he added, "With all of that said, we want to give you an opportunity to hear from our new, interim President and CEO of Universal Systems, Jack Alexander."

Jack stood, made his way to the lectern, shook hands with Shane, and then looked out at the media and Universal employees. When the applause subsided, he said, "Where did you all come from?"

When the polite laughter died down, Jack spoke again. "First, I need to express my deepest sympathy to Lenard Shapiro and his family. I am thankful nothing more serious happened to him. As I told him and the board, I only plan to take over this role until Len is healthy and returns. He is the only CEO of Universal Systems I have ever known. He has led this company in a superior fashion. He is not only a great leader but a terrific friend."

As he finished uttering his final words, a hand went up in the middle of the room. He pointed to the person and said, "Yes, you have a question?"

"I'm Janet Michaelson from the *Tribune*. How long do you anticipate Lenard Shapiro being out?"

"We don't exactly know at this point. It is really a question of how quickly his injuries heal."

"Yes, but what is your best guesstimate at this point?"

Jack gripped the lectern tightly with both hands. There was a slight strain on his face as he glanced down. Then he relaxed by smiling broadly and looked at the reporter and responded, "Your guess would be as good as mine. After a severe car accident, there are injuries both physical and psychological. Right now, it is tough to say."

Another hand went up. He directed his attention to the media person. "You have a comment or a question?"

"Well, with this change, how will it impact your stock price?"

Jack had anticipated this question and was ready for it. "Our stock price is strong. It is based on several factors: our strong service to our clients, their satisfaction with the job we are doing, our strong working relationships with them, and ultimately, our solutions to their business problems."

"Yes, but without your CEO, won't your stockholders get nervous and possibly start to dump your shares?"

He was quick to answer. "Let me assure you, the performance of our company and our stock price have been strong for several quarters. We haven't lost our CEO; he is just laid up for a while as he heals. If I should need any advice on urgent matters that stump me, I'll be able to consult with Len. So, this is a little speed bump in the grand scheme of things."

There were more questions and Jack adroitly handled them all. After they started to become somewhat redundant. Jack said, "Thank you for all for coming. Right now, we must get back to the work we need to do for our clients, employees, and shareholders. Again, thank you for coming."

With his last comment, the press conference was over. It took a while for the room to clear. Shane asked Jack, "Can we walk over to your office? I have a couple of things I need to cover with you."

"No problem."

Shane McCarthy had been the Board Chairman of Universal Systems for four years. Len knew him from years prior when they'd worked together. Len and Shane had maintained a relationship for more than ten years. Len trusted him and often he would ask his opinion regarding difficult decisions. So, when the previous Board Chairman stepped down, Len asked him to fill the role. Shane was in his fifties. He was five foot ten but looked shorter. At least ten years before, he had started to lose his hair. Now he only had a small crop of hair just above his ears. He was slightly overweight, and his puffy Irish face would become beet red, especially when he was angry or flustered. He was almost cross-eyed. Yet, he had one of the sharpest minds Len had ever encountered. As a result, Len had come to rely on his wisdom and advice.

After they sat down in his office, Shane said, "Nice job out there. You handled the media as if you had done it a couple hundred times."

Jack knew he hadn't asked to talk to him simply to praise him for the way he handled the press conference. He asked him directly, "So, what did you want to discuss?"

Jack looked directly at him without blinking.

Shane didn't disappoint. He spoke right up. "The board is concerned about the stock price. It is our opinion this interim change will negatively impact it. There are those in the market, specifically those financial institutions holding large shares of Universal, who are nervous right now. When Universal missed its forecast last year, there was also some apprehension in the market. Now with this change, there is a feeling the stock is not a stable investment."

Jack listened intently. His face was relaxed. It showed no signs of the anxiety building inside him. He was uncomfortable with the board's attitude toward his boss and friend. It was clear they were more concerned with the stock's performance than Len's health. The longer he droned on, the angrier Jack became. But he didn't display any of it. Finally, he said, "Shane, I have seen the new three-year plan. It's rock solid."

Shane didn't respond. Jack watched him look out the window at Lake Michigan. There were a few boats in the water. While it was a nice day, off in the distance was evidence of approaching storm clouds. Jack saw him turn toward him. "You are probably right. The board is curiously waiting for the plans you and the rest of the leadership team put together. Nonetheless, one of our opinions is to quickly move to a position of stability and name a permanent successor to Len's role. We think this will send a strong message to the industry, Universal's clients, and the media. We all concur the most obvious choice should be you."

Jack almost jumped out of his chair. He wanted to shout, yell, and scream at him, *"You and the rest of the board must be insane. We have had years of great success under Len's leadership. Now because of one bad year and Len's accident, you want to dump him like a bad habit."* Even so, he managed to control his emotions. He looked at Shane as if he had just been told they were going to his favorite restaurant. He replied, "What? This makes no sense!"

"Look, we know where your allegiances lie. But if you decide to take a hard stand on this, the board will immediately move to retain a search firm to find Len's replacement. Again, we would prefer the replacement be you. But we will move forward either way. You really need to think about your decision. As you know, it takes years for a divisional leader to become CEO. Also, if we hire a new CEO, the person will want to bring in their own team. You could very well find yourself demoted or looking for a new job elsewhere."

Jack realized this was not a negotiation. He was being informed of the decision the board had already made. Now it was time for him to develop a strategy. "The board wants an answer and I need a few days to think about this."

Shane crossed his legs, put his hands in a steepled position. After a few seconds of reflection, he replied, "You're right, this is a big deal for you. Okay, take a few days to consider what we talked about. The announcement today actually buys us some time. Rushing is not our objective here."

Jack noticed him look down at his watch; he then said, "I've actually got another meeting to get to. Send me an email with your answer."

Recognizing the meeting was over, he stood at the exact moment Shane did. They shook hands and Jack said, "No problem."

Shane headed toward the door, opened it, and turned back. "Just so you know, we like Len. He has been our go-to guy for years. We have depended on him to make Universal a world-class company. He has always come through. But no relationship lasts forever. Remember, it's not personal, it's just business."

He then turned, walked out the door, and disappeared down the hallway. Jack was left alone with his thoughts. *"CEO of Universal…if I weren't so loyal, I would snap up the role in a heartbeat. It was hard enough for me to take over the role on an interim basis. Now, take over the job permanently? There are three people I need to talk to before I make my next move: Len, Gloria, and Clarence. If they all concur, then maybe I'll consider the CEO position, but not before."*

CHAPTER
SIX

CLARENCE WALKED OUT OF THE Chicago FBI offices like someone in a fog. He couldn't believe the events over the last two hours. He walked into a room thinking he was going to a meeting that turned into his birthday celebration. Just as he got use to the idea, he was marched to the Inspection Division's Internal Investigations Section and accused of a phony sexual abuse charge. His original intention was to walk into the parking garage, get in his car, and drive home. Then it hit him. *"What am I going to tell my wife? She's going to ask why I didn't call to tell her, why I was delayed, and was a no-show for dinner. She had planned to take me out for my birthday. What will she say when I tell her I have been charged with sexual harassment? Tonight's going to be a long night."*

It was after six p.m. The sun had already started descending in the west. As he walked aimlessly through the neighborhood he'd driven in countless times, it occurred to him this was the westside ghetto. There were not many new homes in this area. The area had seen its better days. The farther he went from the Chicago FBI Offices, the more destitute the neighborhood appeared. If he had walked east, he would eventually run into the University of Illinois at Chicago and the hospital complex of Rush Memorial. This area had been gentrified and the price point for homes and condos was astronomical. This was not the case where Clarence now wandered. There was litter scattered all over, every place other than in the garbage cans. The cans that did have garbage in them were overflowing from neglect by the city. Stray dogs and cats ran freely looking for any signs of food to eat. As the sun continued its downward movement to meet the horizon, a marvelous array of colors could be seen in the sky. It was as if God was reminding humanity, He had a tremendous plan for each day. As one day came to an end, the sunset was His way of saying, "Look at this array and know I promise to show up again tomorrow with new plans exceeding what you are witnessing now." The problem for Clarence was, he was consumed with his own personal struggles. He wasn't embracing the amazing end-of-day promise. He was feeling and thinking much like the people in this beat-down community. He knew he didn't deserve Director Hammer's scorn. He had a superb record with the FBI; now this. He stopped walking and stood in the middle of a block. Right then, he decided, *"This is not going to break me down. I know the allegations aren't true. It is almost a blessing I was put on administrative leave."* With new determination, he turned around, walked back to the parking lot, got in his car, plugged in his phone, and dialed his wife.

****

Julie answered the phone and started in with a series of questions. "You told me you would be home early so we could go out to a restaurant with the kids and celebrate your birthday. Now that they are in high school, it's tough for us to do anything with them. This was important! What happened? And why did you not tell me about this birthday party in your office? I didn't find out until your boss showed up at our front door. You've got some explaining to do, Mister."

Clarence knew he would have to fill in all the blank spaces over the last two hours. He wasn't looking forward to it, but he knew it would be necessary. So, he started with, "Honey, I'm sorry. There's lots to tell you and I can't do it now. Give me thirty minutes and I'll be home. I promise."

Julie didn't respond right away. Clarence had come to appreciate her ability to try to consider her options before speaking. Finally, she said, "It's probably too late to go out to dinner now. You just come on home, and we will have dinner here."

"Great, see you when I get there. I love you."

"I love you too."

Clarence hung up and immediately started anticipating the conversation he would have with her. He wasn't sure how she would react to the charges, but he knew, in the end, she would support him. From the very beginning of their relationship, she'd always trusted him. In college, there were always tons of people, especially women, around him. He made it clear, after they started dating, he only had eyes for her. They enjoyed being in each other's company. From the time Jack introduced them, they'd spent all their free time with each other. Clarence had never had a girlfriend. So, dating Julie was a new experience for him. He got a few pointers from Jack, but mostly, he figured it out as he went along. Their junior year in college, he went home with her, and she introduced him to her parents. She was from Grand Rapids, Michigan. They liked him immediately. The letters she wrote home helped. She told them how much of a gentleman he was and how he cared for her heart.

During the visit, Julie's father asked Clarence to take a walk through the Gerald R. Ford Museum. As they walked through the museum, Julie's dad said, "My daughter really likes you. She has called us and sent emails about the relationship she has with you. Honestly, she hasn't expressed interest in anyone else as she has with you."

Clarence was quick to reply. "Julie's great, I like Julie a lot!" He looked at Julie's dad and said, "I'm glad I was able to come and meet you and her mother. My father always says, 'It's important to meet the parents of any woman you become interested in'."

"Huh, one day I'd like to meet him."

Clarence hesitated as they continued to walk through the museum. Eventually, he spoke up. "Sir, I have a question for you."

"Okay."

"I am interested in being with Julie for the rest of my life. I haven't asked her, but I wanted to find out from you if you would consent to me marrying your daughter?"

The question took her father completely off guard. He stammered for a bit and then asked, "Are you sure? And are you certain what her answer will be?"

"Well, yes and no, but I'm willing to take my chances."

Her dad was floored by how certain he was about his daughter. He replied, "If she agrees to your marriage proposal, you will have our blessing. Have you thought about what you would do if she said 'No'?"

"Nope."

He did ask her. With a ring in hand and down on one knee, he proposed to her, and she said, "Yes." They were engaged until they graduated and then had a June wedding. Clarence continued to say it was the best decision he ever made.

So, as he thought about the impending conversation with Julie, he had some jitters, but he knew he could trust in her to stand by him.

They had an enjoyable dinner with their children. They gave him gifts he appreciated, and then they went off to bed. Afterwards, Clarence explained the entire situation to Julie.

She sat and listened to everything without stopping him. When he finished, she said, "Honey, this whole thing will blow over. They will come to find out this is all bogus. I have complete faith in you."

"Thanks, babe."

"What do you need from me?"

Clarence thought about her question and just how fortunate he was to have a loving, supportive wife like Julie. He replied, "I don't need you to do anything. In truth, just hearing you ask that is more than enough."

"Great. It's time for us to get to bed. Happy birthday! I'm so sorry it wasn't a better one."

"Hey, no worries...I love you."

CHAPTER

SEVEN

JACK WAITED FOR HIS WIFE to pick up his call. When the connection was made, he heard her voice.

"J, thanks for calling me. I was wondering when I should start cooking. When are you planning to get home?"

He answered her question with a question. "Hey, G, how are you, babe?"

Jack and Gloria had used 'J' and 'G' as nicknames almost from the time they started dating. Lately, life was good for them. Things had settled down significantly over the last few years. They had raised their kids and felt great about each of them being on their own. Gloria had worked in banking for several years. While she had excelled and been promoted multiple times, she had a disdain for managing money. She loved the people part but not the rest of it. The two of them worked it out so she could leave the corporate world and open a successful flower-arranging business. In addition, it gave her the opportunity to spend more time with her aging parents and mentor women leaders.

A few years back, when Jack was kidnapped, Gloria was the prayer warrior who believed God would rescue her husband and bring him back to her. FBI Special Agent Harper and Detective McClain from the Chicago police department headed up the team responsible for rescuing him. Ever since then, Jack and Gloria never missed an opportunity to say "I love you" at the end of the night or the end of a phone call. They learned to appreciate their relationship.

"I needed to call you because there have been some new developments and I need to go visit Len at the hospital. It turns out the board is planning to dump Len and permanently replace him."

There was silence on the phone for several seconds. Finally, Gloria said, "How messed up is that?"

"They think his time is coming to an end. They are likely going to find a new CEO."

Gloria wasted no time in speaking up. "So, what now?"

"Well, that's what I want to talk to Len about. I've got more to tell you, but I need to go see him now, so I won't get home too late, okay?"

Again, Gloria was silent. Yet, she had a way of being able to discern things Jack was holding onto. With the few things he had shared, she decided not to press him. "Okay, do what you have to do."

"See you before eight o'clock tonight."

"Got it…love you."

"Love you, too."

As Gloria hung up, she offered up a prayer. "Lord, continue to watch over my husband and keep him safe. Oh yeah, continue to heal Len. Amen."

****

Jack pulled his car into an open parking place at the Evanston hospital. He sat in the car for a few minutes collecting his thoughts. Earlier, when he called Len to tell him he was coming by to see him, Len asked a few questions. Jack didn't give him real fulsome answers. He said he would cover the details in person. He had tried to sound light and yet matter of fact. He didn't want to reveal his true feelings over the phone. As he got out of the car, he reflected on something his mother had told him years ago: *It is not a question of whether trials and difficulties will arise in life. The question is how you respond to them.*

"Len, how are you doing, my friend?"

Len's foot was still in a cast and hoisted above his head. The doctors still had him under observation because of the severe concussion. He was in a private room and had several amenities, including a 52" surround sound TV. When he saw Jack walk into the room, he immediately turned off the television.

"Jack, you need to get some new lines. Still in a cast, still in the hospital, and still eating bad food."

"Got it."

"Now tell me what's going on, the things you weren't telling me on the phone. Oh, and don't leave anything out."

After Jack shared everything with him, Len sat up in bed and asked Jack to pull his chair closer.

"You've been like a son to me over all these years. There's been some adversity, but we have always found ways to overcome it and make Universal a success. Now there's going to be a changing of the guard, this much is clear. I won't be the Leader of the Pack anymore. I am going to give you some specific directions. My hope is you will follow them to the letter. If you do, things will work out to your highest good. So, listen carefully. In fact, I strongly recommend you take notes. "

As Jack walked back to his car, he realized again the wisdom of Len. He had told Jack the exact moves he needed to make. He tried to capture the relevant points and direction Len provided. His mind was swirling, so much so that he never noticed the dark black Mercedes in the parking lot just three cars away from him or the two men in the car watching him. As he got out on the road to go home, the car managed to stay a safe distance behind Jack's car so they wouldn't be noticed. They apparently knew where he lived, because when he turned down his street before the garage opened, they headed in a different direction.

****

Clarence decided the first thing he needed to do was get information from Agent Landers about the allegation. He had to get to the bottom of this quickly. He determined this was all a big misunderstanding. He also knew he couldn't talk to her himself since there was an open investigation. He had to find someone who could talk to her without drawing attention to him. He racked his brain and couldn't come up with anyone in the Bureau. Additionally, he knew any access on his part to her file would be an automatic red flag to Internal Investigations. Then it came to him, the one person he could trust to help him. He immediately got in his car and drove to a cell phone store. He bought four burner phones. He didn't want to use his own phone and he couldn't use his cell phone from the Bureau. So, he activated one of the phones, put two in a bag and then dialed his intended number. When he made connection, he gave some simple instructions where the person was to go and pick up a package he was going to leave there. He said there would be instructions inside.

Clarence left the package in the designated spot and walked away. He found a secluded location, sat down, and waited for his newly acquired cell phone to ring. Twenty-five minutes passed, forty minutes passed, and when his watch showed forty-six minutes, the exact time in his instructions, his phone rang.

"Hey, my friend, thanks for calling me. When forty-five minutes passed, I started to worry."

"I'm told FBI agents never worry."

"I worried you were still using your old flip phone to tell time, or you were still wearing your old Timex. You know, 'takes a licking but keeps on ticking'."

"Ha ha…Clarence, you are funny, still making jokes. Now that we have finished all your cloak and dagger stuff, what's up? You know I've got a company to run."

"Yeah, I heard…interim CEO of Universal. So, somebody is moving up in the world. How's the weather up there?"

"Are we done with you trying to be a comedian? What's going on? Why couldn't we simply meet at Starbucks?"

Over the next thirty minutes, Clarence explained the situation. Since he was talking to his best friend, he left nothing out. Jack got to ask every possible question. Eventually, he asked Clarence a final question. "So, what do you need me to do?"

"Well, the way I figure it, Agent Landers has to have a mighty good reason for making such an outlandish allegation. Someone must be putting some extreme pressure on her. I need to find out who and why. That's where you come in. As CEO of Universal, whether interim or not, you have the capacity to dig into Agent Landers' information and find out what's behind all this."

Jack listened intently. He was following everything Clarence said until he mentioned Agent Landers' information. He interrupted him and said, "Wait, wait, you're asking for something I can't deliver."

"No, no, I'm not suggesting you break into FBI files. I'm talking about her personal information, emails, phone calls, especially text messages, anything to give us a clue as to what this is all about. I know what I'm asking you to do borders on ethics issues. But I am fighting for my life and my reputation here. If you decide to refuse, I will understand, I simply can't do this on my own."

There was an extended period of silence on the phone. Jack was thinking on all he had heard, and Clarence was waiting for Jack's response. Jack thought back over his long-standing relationship with his friend, in college, after graduation, the whistle-blowing event he'd helped him with, and how he'd saved his life when he was kidnapped. He realized there wasn't anything he wouldn't do or try to do for him. Finally, he spoke. "Okay, okay, I will definitely help you get to the bottom of this. Whatever it takes, I'll have to work it out. You obviously need help, and I can try to help you. I'm not sure how to go about it."

CHAPTER
EIGHT

TWO MEN SAT IN A late model Cadillac. The car was parked in a half-empty parking lot towards the back and out of sight.

"Well, did you take care of it?"

"Hey, I'm the master at this!"

"It must not be traceable to our source."

"Not a chance. There is no bank, email address, contact, or electronic reference point. It was deposited like we agreed."

"And the amount?"

"Eleven point four million into his account. He will try and deny any knowledge of the funds. But he will be caught red-handed."

"Good. Now we'll just sit and wait. Between the sexual harassment charge and this payoff , he will have no recourse but to resign, if they don't convict him first."

"Right!"

"Okay, get out of here and don't contact me unless something goes wrong."

****

Jack got in his car after walking back from the spot where Clarence had placed the burner phone. The conversation was very revealing. His buddy was in trouble. Jack thought, *"Why in the world would anyone want to frame him? He is a real stand-up citizen, an honorable FBI agent, a terrific husband and father. Motivation…what's the motivation for this? I don't know, but I will do everything in my power to help him. I can't start digging through someone else's personal information to try and find some answers. I'm not skilled in this area. Even if he gave me a three-month tutorial, I still would be inept. Maybe I agreed too quickly. I probably need to call him back and tell him…wait a minute. I think I might have a solution. If I can't do it, maybe there is someone who can."*

****

"Mr. Shapiro, we've checked your injuries and we've reviewed your recent MRI. Based on our assessment, you are well enough to leave, free to check out. The nurse will come in later and go over your outpatient care. You need to stay home for the next three to four weeks. But you don't need to spend any more time here in the hospital. We will need to see you back here in three weeks for a follow-up examination. But we will be releasing you today."

Len was surprised and elated. He was more than ready to go home, give up eating hospital food, and try to re-adapt to regular life.

"Doc, thanks for helping me break out of here. I owe you a dinner for you and your wife or some tickets to your favorite sporting event. You just gave me my life back."

40

"Mr. Shapiro, I don't need anything from you. Your health is compensation enough. Just look for the nurse with your instructions and medications. Have a great day."

"Thanks again, Doc."

Len wasn't sure if he should try to jump up and click his heels or spit against the wall. With a cast on both his leg and arm, spitting was probably a better choice. He was thankful to be leaving the hospital. However, he couldn't go back to work. The board had given the reins of the company to Jack and that was just the precursor to making him the permanent CEO. It appeared he didn't have a role in Universal anymore. Like it or not, he was being put out to pasture. His choices were to fight the decision, negotiate his severance and start looking for another job, or simply retire early. He knew his wife would want him to choose the latter. Based on his investment portfolio, he didn't have to work another day in his life. As he sat there considering his options, he realized if the car accident hadn't happened, he would still be CEO, albeit working through the turnaround issue. Then he stopped and sat back in his bed. He looked up at the ceiling and thought, *"Wait a minute, the car accident, was it my mishap or was my car purposely sabotaged? Jack said he was having someone check it out. I wonder what he found?"*

Lenard Shapiro had been CEO of Universal Systems for multiple years. He was a fair but no-nonsense guy. To Jack, he *looked* like a CEO. He was six foot two, a full head of dark hair, with strong, dark brown eyes. He was in great shape. Jack found out later that he worked out just about every day, a combination of running and weightlifting. He spoke in a manner that let you know he was always in control. However, this accident had left him feeling vulnerable. Nothing like this had ever happened to him in his life.

After getting his undergraduate degree, he had wanted to be a high school history teacher. Studying the world, various cultures, and how they all fit together was a passion of his. It was his father who suggested he get a master's degree to earn more money. When he took the GMAT (Graduate Management Admissions Test), he scored so high his career counselor suggested he consider the law. After he spent some time with his old high school history teacher, he was convinced to take the LSAT. The Law School Admission Test was a real challenge. However, he did well. So, he decided to apply for law school. He was accepted, and when he graduated and passed the bar, he was sought after by several firms based on his interest in business law. Throughout the process, he remembered the words of his old history teacher, "You can take a law degree into any profession you choose."

He selected a firm to work for and then one promotion led to another. He moved up the ranks slowly at first and then started to gain momentum. He held senior leadership positions with three different firms before he was recruited to take over the top spot at Universal Systems. By that time, he was married and had two children. His wife Ilana understood the realities of his work as a senior executive for major corporations. His travels and late-night meetings came with the territory. He tried to be home as much as possible to watch his kids grow up. It was a difficult balance; in the end, his corporate responsibilities associated with revenue, profit, and shareholder value won out.

****

Jack hit the speed dial for his intended number, and it was picked up immediately.

"Hey, my friend. You must need something. I'm guessing this isn't a social call."

"Fred, I need your help."

"Okay, like what?"

There was an extended pause on the line. Then Jack spoke up. "When can we meet?"

Fred and Jack agreed on a time and place. Jack was concerned about the privacy factor. So, he had him come to the floor at Universal used only for extra-private meetings. There were separate entrances and private exit doors. When Fred arrived, Jack was already in the room and sitting at a small conference table.

Fred took a seat. "Okay, you got me here. Now what is so darn important, secret, and urgent?

Jack spent the next hour explaining the details. Fred asked several questions, and Jack did his best to address every one of them. When the conversation had reached a conclusion, he sat back in his chair, looked at Fred, and said, "Can you do it?"

Fred took an inordinate amount of time looking over the extensive notes he'd taken. He scratched his nose and rubbed his eyes with the palms of his hands. This was his habit when he was wrestling over a decision. Finally, he put his pen down on top of his notes, took a deep breath, and then looked Jack squarely in the face and said, "Yes I can."

Jack then said, "Two questions. How long will it take and what will you need from me?"

Fred didn't hesitate. "Look, for a list of things I'll need, you and I can never email or text each other. We will need to use burner throw-away phones. I brought a phone for you with a password."

Jack took both the phone and a sheet of paper with some letters and numbers on it.

"Memorize my burner phone number and your password. Never write any of this down. I will call you and tell you where and when to bring the things I need."

"Can you get what I need in a week?"

"Jack, you will be the only person I can ever communicate with throughout this process. If you violate any portion of our agreement, I will not provide you with any information at all. Do we have an agreement?"

He looked at Fred and said, "Absolutely, I agree one hundred percent.."

He watched Fred as he struck a match, lit the paper on fire. He let the ash fall pnto a small aluminum foil sheet and then put the contents in his pocket.

"Okay, wait for my text message with the list."

Jack let Fred out a private entrance. Then he sat down and reflected on the meeting he'd just had. Fred Russell was a guy he could trust. He thought back to how they'd met. Fred owned his own security and surveillance company. When Jack had first become President of JPC and had to travel overseas without Gloria, he had received threatening anonymous letters. He was concerned for Gloria's safety.

Clarence had recommended Fred and his company. "Fred is the best. I would trust him with my life and the lives of my family. Plus, if you ever need someone to do some undercover work, he's your guy. He is actually better than most of the special agents in the FBI."

He relied on Clarence's recommendation, and he never worried about Gloria's safety during his absences. Jack wondered why Clarence didn't suggest using Fred.

****

"Honey, how are you feeling? I know you didn't like being held up in the hospital. The doctor gave you the okay to leave, but I want to know how you feel mentally. So much has happened to you. I know when you called to tell me you had been in a car crash; I was a wreck. So, I know you must be feeling something."

"I'm not real talkative, let's just get home."

"Got it, but once all of this settles down, I need to process this whole thing with you. Don't shut me out. Agreed?"

"No problem."

"The kids are still in town. You should expect them to be inquisitive and hovering once we get home. So, you need to be prepared for it."

Once they drove into the driveway, Len's two sons came out to the car and helped their father into the house. They were particularly careful since he still had the cast on his leg. They were ecstatic to finally see him. Yet, they were concerned for his overall health. Almost in unison, they asked, "Dad, how are you feeling? Okay, watch out for the steps. Where would you like to sit, in the den, the living room, or upstairs in your bedroom? Can we get you something to eat or drink? We want you to know we are at your beck and call."

Len was thankful for all the attention. Being cooped up in the hospital for so long was not pleasant. He said, "Look, I'm so happy to see you. Thank you for flying in to be with me. You are a sight for sore eyes. Your mother and I talked on the way home. This cast is a bit restrictive,

45

and I am still in some pain, despite the meds they have me on. Your mom and I were thinking of having a light dinner together, if I am up to it. But right now, I need you to help me upstairs to our bedroom , okay?"

His sons said, "Dad, no worries. You just let us know what's best for you. At some point, we want to hear what happened to you in the car."

With help, Len slowly walked up the stairs to the master bedroom. As he sat in a chair staring off into space and at the cast on his leg, he realized, for the first time in his life, he was afraid, for himself, his family, and his position with the company he had given much of his life to. His thoughts wandered to; *"I've got to get in touch with Jack. I'm sure by now he's found out whether my car was tampered with. And if it was, why would anyone want to screw around with my car? What would be their motivation? I've got to call him."*

CHAPTER

NINE

THERE WEREN'T MANY CARS ON the street yet. Jack liked to get his run in while the rest of the world was still asleep or just waking up. As he headed north along his favorite route. He glanced to his right and saw the beginnings of the sun starting to come up. Before the bright sunny globe appeared, he saw shades of orange, apricot, yellow, and red, separated while still together. It was if God was saying, "Wake up, look, and see what I have planned for you today." He tried to keep his eyes on the road in front of him. Nonetheless, he couldn't help but look over at the sun's efforts to reveal itself to the world. He reached his turnaround point and started running even harder. This was his way of challenging himself to finish his run faster than his previous times. He always had a song in his head that matched the cadence of his running steps. He picked up his pace as the song dominated his thoughts. With just a half mile to go, he took his last look at the sun which had now risen above the horizon. The yellow, orange globe seemed to be changing in its intensity every second, much like the intensity of Jack's last half mile. He finished the last 300 yards as fast as he could, as if he were running in the Olympics. He was totally out of breath, huffing and puffing like he was ready to fall over. This was the way he finished every run. It gave him great satisfaction to know he had given it his all. He walked slowly back to his house, trying to recover his normal breathing pattern. As he did, his thoughts led him to the current concerns he was facing. He thought, *"It seems there is so much swirling around me, people need my help, so much I am being asked to do. Clarence is in real trouble. I can't abandon him after all he's done for me. He saved my life, for goodness' sake. I pray I have found a great resource in Fred who can help. Then Len asked me to step in and be interim CEO. And if that weren't enough, now the board wants me to be the permanent guy. Yeah, I'm honored but my allegiance is to Len. Poor guy laid up in the hospital. Now they want to take him out like yesterday's trash. I still haven't found out the real cause of his accident. All these people, all these issues. I guess I must plod through this believing I can come up with real solutions. I've got to just take them one at a time."*

As Jack walked back home, he didn't notice the black Cadillac sedan parked a block behind him. He also didn't notice it had been there ever since he had reached his turnaround point and started heading back home.

****

Jack walked into his house, went to the kitchen to get some cool water. The house felt empty since Gloria had taken the last few days to spend with her elderly mother. He walked into his study and hit the Enter key to his computer. As he waited for the screen, he picked up his phone, scrolled through his text messages and stopped at one with great interest.

> **You need to call me back as soon as you can. I have an urgent issue.**

Jack reflected on the text for a moment. As he quickly looked through the others, he stopped again at a text that only said,

When I thought things couldn't get any worse, they just go miserably out of control. We need to talk.

He decided it would be best to immediately respond to the first text.

Got it! I will reach out to you this morning. What's the topic?

A text message came right back.

I need you to call me. Make sure you call me on the right phone.

Jack's only reply was,

Okay!

He went back to the second text and replied,

I have one thing I need to address and then I will call you. Is that soon enough?

He waited for a reply, which came quickly.

Thanks for not leaving me dangling. I'll be waiting for your call.

Jack felt a bit overwhelmed. Nevertheless, he fully realized he didn't have time to be consumed with his own feelings. He quickly showered, shaved, dressed, and sat down at his desk in his home office. He took a fast pass through his other text and email messages. He then texted his executive assistant, Beth, to reschedule any appointments he had for the next two hours and for her to address any other urgent business. Afterwards, he looked at the first text again for a few seconds before dialing a number. The phone was answered immediately.

"Thanks for calling me."

He sensed the desperation in Len's voice. This was an emotion he had never encountered with Len before. He had expressed anxiety or signs of frustration but never desperation.

"Len, what's up?"

There was silence on the line momentarily. Then Len spoke. "Did you find out what happened with my car? What caused the accident besides me getting lost in my thoughts? Was there some foul play in anyway?"

Jack collected his thoughts before responding. Then he said, "I don't know the answer. I have someone I trust checking out your car completely."

"Answers, answers...I need answers!"

Jack could tell there was nothing he could say that would quell Len's anxiety. He was as amped up as he was when they first started talking. He started slowly. "Len, what's going on for you right now? Why so agitated?"

Len didn't speak right away. However, he could tell Len's breathing over the phone had become more regulated. Then he heard Len say, "I'm freaking out right now. If someone tampered with my car, will they be coming after me and my wife next?"

Now Jack's mind was moving a hundred miles a minute. *"Was there some foul play? Why would anyone try and hurt Len? What would be the motivation? What had he done that was so egregious?"* He was buried in his thoughts when he heard, "Are you following me?"

"I thought by now I would already know. I'll call you back."

CHAPTER
TEN

J ACK ENDED HIS CALL AS another text message popped up.

Are you free now? I really need to talk to you.

He dialed the number and waited. Only a few seconds elapsed before the call connected.

"Somebody has it in for me. This whole thing has got me reeling. If I can't figure this out, soon my career and my family will be negatively impacted. I've got to get—"

"Hold on, my friend. You need to slow way down. I have never heard you spun up like this. You sound like a madman."

He waited. He could only hear fast, rapid, and heavy breathing on the line. Little by little, he could tell Clarence's breathing became more stable. Nonetheless, he could hear some faint mumbling. Then he heard Clarence speak. "The Bureau is now accusing me of taking bribes. I've never taken a bribe in my life!"

Jack was stunned by what he heard. "A bribe?"

"Over eleven million dollars showed up in an off-shore account traced back to me as the owner."

"Really?"

Jack heard him take another deep breath before answering. Then he said, "It just came up this morning. When I asked how this was supposedly discovered, I was told they received an anonymous tip."

"An anonymous tip…other than this *mysterious tip*, what else ties you to this? "

"That's the point, no one will tell me anything. Their line is the same one I've used a thousand times, 'I can't comment on anything associated with an open investigation.' So, I'm stuck. If I can't get clear of this and the sexual harassment charges, I could be fired, prosecuted, and convicted. Now I have been suspended indefinitely. I was told any of my actions or associations during the suspension can and will have a negative impact on my case. So, unfortunately, we can't even be seen together until this whole thing is over."

Jack was quick to reply. "Okay, seeing you is the least of our worries right now."

He heard Clarence speak calmly for the first time in the conversation. "I thought our guy who's looking into the sexual harassment claims could get eyes on this situation as well."

"You mean hacking the FBI's database to determine specifically what they have on you? Maybe there is someone in the Bureau you trust who can help us get the intel we need. If we can help it, let's not get you in to deeper waters than you already are."

"Yes, so before you go any further, my friend, I need you to consider the costs."

Jack now heard in Clarence a calm, steady voice. There were no signs of anxiety. He seemed like the level-headed guy he had come to know. Jack reflected on what he was told and realized the significance of his words. Nevertheless, he remembered the importance of his relationship with his buddy. Again, this was the man who'd saved his life. It was then he realized he had to do all he could to help save him. He responded with, "My friend, let's pick a strategy and then let's do this."

CHAPTER
ELEVEN

FROM A HOTEL A BLOCK from Water Tower Place, on the Magnificent Mile, north of downtown Chicago, a woman with an enormous hat and sunglasses stepped out into 70-degree weather and walked toward Michigan Avenue. She was stylishly dressed in a radiant summer outfit. Her blonde hair and pale skin seemed to fit in with many of the people out enjoying the day. She sauntered about a half block west, turned the corner at a traffic light and got into the backseat of a Cadillac sedan with tinted windows and plates registered to a deceased man in upstate New York. The driver took a circuitous route and eventually got on Lake Shore Drive heading north. The woman said nothing as she looked out her window at Lake Michigan. The lake had three shades of blue; near the shoreline there was a lighter shade of blue because of the impact of the sand. The water took on a darker shade as her view moved away from the shoreline, out one hundred yards. Despite the fact the other side of the lake could not be seen, the dark, rich blue of the water was so evident as she took it all in. While there were a few boats moving in different directions, none of them seemed to be in a hurry.

There was a sea of humanity on the lake shore, bike riders, walkers, volleyball players, and others on blankets enjoying the sun's radiance. She thought to herself, *"Even from Lake Shore Drive, the smell of suntan lotion is more evident than gasoline."* As the car passed Oak Street Beach at 45 miles an hour, she could hear faint sounds of laughter from people enjoying themselves.

There was a much more somber mood inside the car as it continued north. For the first time since getting in the car on Michigan Avenue, Catherine turned away from the window and looked at the other passenger sitting next to her who had been on the phone the entire time. The first words she heard when the phone call ended were, "So, what's the latest update? And what yet needs to be done?"

****

Jack called Beth, his executive assistant, and cleared the rest of the items on his calendar for the day. After he finished, he sat back, consumed in his thoughts. *"This cannot be a coincidence. Two of the most important people to me are reeling from life-changing issues. In addition, they both are asking for my help. If I make the slightest misstep, we could all fall like a house of cards. One option could be to do nothing, simply sit back, and watch them slip into a giant abyss. Lord knows I can't do that. I've got to do everything I can to help. If they go down, I guess I'll go down with them."*

****

"I had my guys go over the car multiple times. Then I went back over it myself, just to be sure."

Jack listened on the phone and took notes so he could remember every detail. With his pen poised, he said, "Let's hear it."

"The car had definitely been tampered with. It was done by an absolute professional. Small things were done and would be missed by the average mechanic. If you hadn't asked me to look for possible sabotage, *we* may have even missed them."

This piqued Jack's interest. "Missed what?"

"I could tell you all of the minute details, but the essential things you need to know are these: the brakes were definitely tampered with, the steering wheel was too, and there were things done to at least two of the car tires. One way or another, the car was doomed to fail in a big way. Your friend is fortunate to still be alive."

He was shocked by what he heard. His hand was shaking so much, he couldn't hold the pen in his hand. He thought, *"who would do such an evil, foul, intentional thing? Len doesn't have any enemies he's ever told me about. What is going on here?"*

"Jack, are you still there?"

He snapped back from his thoughts. "Yes, yes, do me a favor and email your entire report to my personal email address. And one more thing…don't repeat what you told me to anyone. You would be potentially placing yourself in harm's way."

CHAPTER

TWELVE

A **FEW YEARS HAD PASSED** since Catherine Frazier had orchestrated the kidnapping of Jack Alexander. She was regretful she hadn't had a better plan associated with his demise. The plan seemed flawless. He was thrown into a car in his building's garage as he was getting out of his own car. The three kidnappers made sure it was clean and timely. The injection into his neck immobilized him as he was driven across the Illinois state line into Wisconsin. It turned out Catherine, dressed up as a man, had been the one who injected Jack in the garage. She got out of the car after he was abducted, changed clothes, and made her way back to her daughter's apartment without being detected. Instead of taking the original payoff for the job, one of the kidnappers got greedy and demanded more money. During the interchange, the Wisconsin state troopers detected the car on the interstate. Special Agent Clarence Harper mobilized his team and with the state police were able to apprehend one of the abductors and later rescue Jack.

Catherine's plan had failed. But she was determined to take him down for being a whistleblower and all the trouble he had caused her. She spent seven long years in a federal penitentiary. She made up her mind she would not rest until she had destroyed Jack Alexander.

She spent more than three years after his rescue building a new plan. Realizing she could not do this on her own, she made several inquiries of people whom she knew while in prison, people she could trust. Eventually, she was led to a man who had far bigger interests than simply taking down one man. Armando Santos, a first-generation Columbian in the United States, was the son of Orlando and Miriam. His parents met, married, and came to the US in search of a better life.

His mother was the youngest of four children. She had two brothers and a sister. Her parents grew up in Cartagena, a Columbian city port. From a young age, she lived in a *Republicano*-style home which represented the independence of Colombian art. This style of home incorporated cement and steel building materials, typically built on a single level with an A-frame roof.

There were only three bedrooms. She shared a room with her sister. And because of the room size, they slept in bunk beds; she had the top bunk which meant she climbed a ladder to get into bed every night.

Life was particularly good for Miriam. She and her siblings went to a public school only three blocks from home. Since she was the youngest, her sister took her to school with her and made sure she brought her home every day.

Her father worked in a furniture factory until she was in high school. This was the same factory her brothers worked in when they finished high school. Her sister got married right out of high school to her childhood sweetheart and moved out of the house. It meant Miriam had the bedroom all to herself. Later, her father stopped working at the factory. She didn't understand what his new job was, but her family started living the "Good Life." Previously, the family never had an automobile. Everyone took *chivas*, the bus, everywhere. Now she got the opportunity to ride in a car. Other things changed as well. Their primary food was the midday meal, lunch. It consisted of rice with coconut, fried plantains, and, on rare occasions, shrimp. His "new" job now afforded them the opportunity to have the best seafood and meats the town could offer. She wondered what the reason was for the job change, but she never asked. Then one day, she overheard her parents talking. Her mother said, "This is not right! We were better off when you worked in the factory. At least it was honest work, and we could hold our heads up in the community. Don't you realize our neighbors know what you do for a living?"

"I worked in that stinking factory for almost twenty years, and we barely had food on the table."

"But it was decent work. Now you put the whole family at risk by being involved in drug smuggling."

"As soon as I get enough money, I'll use it to start my own business."

"Honey, once they have you, they never want to let you go. You need to stop now before you get in too deep."

"I want you and our family to have a better life."

"Not this way."

"I'm not really smuggling drugs. All I do is watch and make sure the shipments get on the right boat. I don't handle any drugs and I'm really not involved in where the shipments go."

"Don't be naïve!"

"If something happens to me, I have enough money saved to take care of you while I'm gone."

"I don't care. You need to stop now before it's too late."

"Okay, in one more year, I promise."

Now Miriam realized what was going on, and why their lifestyle had changed. She didn't know much about drugs except there were those who were involved in drugs and those who were not. She also knew it was against the law. It was at that point she started being concerned about her father's safety.

Something else started happening around the same time. One of her girlfriends at school introduced her to a young man from their high school. Orlando Santos was one year ahead of her in high school. She had seen him around school, but she hadn't paid much attention to him. One event changed all that for Miriam. She was leaving school at the end of the week and a guy from one of her classes approached her and wanted to walk her home. She refused and started walking in the opposite direction. The guy followed her and pulled her arm. He pulled it so hard she fell on the ground.

"You think you're too good to let me walk you home? Really, I would be doing you a favor."

The next thing she knew, Orlando spun the guy around and hit him so hard he fell in a heap. He said, "You've got a lot of nerve hurting Miriam for no reason. It's creeps like you that give guys a bad name. If you ever go near her again, I'll break your jaw."

He turned and helped Miriam up off the ground. He picked up her books and said, "I'm so sorry for what happened to you. That guy is a real jerk. So he doesn't try to hurt you for what I did to him, I'm going to see to it you get home safe. If it's okay with you, I'll see to it you get back and forth to school for a while until you're sure he leaves you alone."

Miriam was so impressed. He was handsome, but he obviously cared about her safety and wellbeing. She agreed to his suggestion, and it began a series of walks for them to and from school. When the next school dance came, Orlando asked her to go, and she agreed. For the rest of high school, the two of them dated and fell in love. Their parents approved of them dating and so they continued.

When high school was over, they both got jobs and started to discuss marriage. Orlando asked her parents if he could marry her; they agreed and after an elaborate ceremony, they got an apartment together.

Months later, Miriam got up the nerve to ask her mother about her father's involvement in drug smuggling. Her mother was surprised Miriam knew about it. Nonetheless, she told her the truth.

"Yes, your father has been involved in this nasty drug-smuggling business. He told me three years ago he would get out and yet he is still in it. I'm afraid for him, and for our family. Your brothers have had the good sense to stay far away from this madness. But the authorities could round us all up for reaping the benefits of drug money. You and Orlando are not safe here. I don't want anything to happen to you."

"Mom, I'm going to talk to Orlando about all this. I think he should know."

"Maybe you should leave here and go someplace else."

Miriam and Orlando talked about the situation that night and made some decisions.

"I don't want anything to happen to you, to us. I'm prepared to not only leave Cartagena, but to leave Colombia."

"Really?

"I have an uncle who works for the US Embassy in Bogota. Also, one of my cousins lives in the United States. I'm sure if I asked him, he would agree to sponsor us."

"The United States?

"Yeah, why not?"

Miriam thought it over for a few days. Then one night over dinner, she said, "Okay, Let's give it a try."

"What?"

"I'm ready to go to the United States. I want a life with you, and I want us to be safe. So, let's do it. I believe we can make it."

Orlando contacted his uncle and wrote to his cousin in the US, and they both agreed to help them. Orlando's family was surprised, but after some discussion, they agreed. Miriam's mother totally supported them leaving the country.

"I want you to be safe. If it means moving to the United States, I agree. And your father will agree with whatever I say."

Within three months, they were on a plane to Chicago. Since Orlando's cousin lived there, it was the perfect place for them. Miriam's parents drove them to the airport. Her mother cried the entire trip. She knew it was the right thing, but she was saying goodbye to her baby girl. Her father was silent as they drove. When he took their bags out of his car, he put an envelope in her carryon bag.

When they went through Customs, she noticed the strange envelope but didn't open it. Once they were in Chicago, she sat in the back seat of the car while Orlando talked to his cousin. She opened the envelope and was shocked to see so much money and a note that read, "*Miriam, your mother told me why you decided to leave Cartagena. Since it's because of me, I decided to give you and Orlando a gift to help you get started in the United States. I love you, Daddy.*"

She cried both from sadness and joy. She waited until they were situated in their new apartment to show Orlando the money and share with him the note from her father. They took the money and established a small typewriter and computer repair company called OMS Corporation. Orlando and Miriam used their first and last initials for the name of the business. Armando's father was highly intelligent, especially in math. He taught himself computer basics and, before long, he was well respected for advanced computer repair. Before long, Orlando started selling computer hardware and software. He focused on providing excellent customer service. People were coming to his store from all over Chicago. Due to their success, they expanded their store by opening two additional Chicago locations. He eventually opened stores in several metropolitan cities.

CHAPTER

THIRTEEN

ARMANDO'S PARENTS MOVED INTO the Humboldt Park community before he was born. It had such a rich mixture of languages and people from different countries. They felt comfortable once they realized Spanish was one of the primary languages in the neighborhood. They only spoke Spanish at home, because they wanted their son to become a part of the fabric of the city. They encouraged him to learn and speak English as well. Grammar school initially was tough for him since English wasn't his primary language at home. His parents found a tutor who helped him learn the language quickly. Before he graduated, they were already determining the high school he would attend. After many discussions with others in the neighborhood, they decided Lane Tech would be the best school for him. He had to apply and take a series of attitude tests. In the end, he passed them with flying colors.

High school was a totally new and different experience for him. None of the kids from his grammar school enrolled at Lane. So, he entered his freshman year having no friends. He felt like he was alone on an isthmus. It likely would have stayed that way, but one incident changed everything. In his English class, he was constantly being made fun of because he had an accent. There were these four or five students who were the ringleaders. The leader of the pack was a guy named Thomas Black. He played sports and was a favorite of the English teacher. Whenever he was called on to answer a question, he would say "Why don't you ask Armando. He's so smart, I'm sure he has the right answer."

Rather than force Thomas to answer the question, the teacher would say, "Okay, Armando, what's the answer to the question?"

Armando was super smart, but he didn't want to say anything for fear he would be laughed at because of his accent. Despite his fears, he spoke up, answered the question, and waited for the teacher's applause. What happened next was laughter from the entire class. While the teacher calmed them down, the damage had been done. After class, he finally confronted Thomas. "I'm putting you on notice, if you ever try to humiliate me again, there will be consequences."

"Consequences…what are you going to do, little Latin boy? Show me your *salsa* dance moves?"

This comment brought new laughter from Thomas' cronies. Armando stood his ground and said, "Let's continue this episode after school today. I'll see you at the soccer field; unless you're too chicken to show up."

"Too chicken…are we talking about food now? Is it Christmas? Are you asking me to show up so you can make some *natillas* or some *arepas?* You Columbian peasants never cease to amaze me. I'll see you after school so we can settle this."

Armando walked away shaking in his shoes. He asked himself, "*What was I expecting him to do, back down? Maybe I let my pride get in the way. Maybe I should have said nothing and just gone on home. But I've got to stand up for myself or this stupid stuff will keep happening. Now I've got to show up. If I don't, this stuff will never end.*"

Armando went to the soccer field after school. He was surprised when he didn't see anyone. The team apparently had no practice. He walked out carrying his bookbag. He stood alone in the middle of the field for three or four minutes. No one showed up. He started to feel relieved and was about to leave when 20 or 30 kids came out of nowhere and started walking toward him. As they got closer, he recognized a few of them from his English class and other classes of his. Apparently, word had spread, and people wanted to see what was going to happen. He could see Thomas surrounded by his little sycophants. They were all smiling and waving their hands. He wasn't sure what was going to happen. But he reflected on the self-defense lessons his father had insisted he take every Saturday. He had never had a fight. He had never seen one, except on television.

Now the other students surrounded him and Thomas. Most of them were yelling. Armando couldn't make out what was being said. But he knew a fight was about to happen and he was the main event. Thomas had a big grin on his face, his head was cocked to one side, and he said, "So, you had some consequences for me. Well, where's the food you brought me? I'm a little hungry."

Adrenaline started running through Armando's body like never before. He calmly walked up to Thomas and reached back like a major league pitcher would before throwing a fast ball. He hit Thomas in his left temple as hard as he could. Thomas was completely caught off guard. His eyes almost came out of their sockets. His head snapped back, and he fell to the ground with a heavy thud. Everyone there stood in shock. Thomas didn't move for a couple of minutes. Armando was just as surprised as everyone else. He stood there wondering where the motivation came from to do what he had just done. Thomas' cronies knelt close to him trying to help him as best they could. He retrieved his bookbag, walked through the crowd, and headed home. He was thankful the bus was coming as he got to the curb. After he paid his fare and sat down, it finally hit him what had transpired; he had had his first fight. He wasn't sure what tomorrow would bring, but the smile on his face reflected the satisfaction he felt inside.

He didn't tell his parents what had happened. As he got off the bus the next day, he half expected to find himself in the principal's office and be told he was suspended for fighting. But as he walked to his locker, students started turning toward him, some were even pointing at him, and still others were whispering. But no one told him to report to the principal's office. Later in the day, he went to his English class. As he walked in and made his way to his desk before the teacher came in, everyone stopped talking and started looking at him. Thomas was already there. He got up and walked over to Armando.

"I owe you an apology. I made you the brunt of my jokes and I shouldn't have. It won't happen again."

From that moment on, he was convinced he could change any situation, accomplish anything he put his mind to, regardless of the odds. While he knew he was an immigrant, he decided he would achieve greatness, regardless of the cost.

CHAPTER
FOURTEEN

HIS PARENTS WERE COMMITTED to giving him the best education possible. After high school, he attended Northwestern University and graduated in the top 10% of his class. Orlando wanted his son to eventually take over the business and grow the OMS brand into a national or even an international enterprise. Armando went to work for his dad after getting a master's degree. Shortly after his arrival, he convinced his dad to turn OMS Corporation into a publicly traded company on the New York Stock Exchange.

Now his vision was to grow by acquisition. He started slowly. He bought other firms to enhance the company's overall portfolio. He was a tough negotiator. Once he made up his mind to acquire a company at a certain price, nothing could stop him. He used every possible tactic to get what he wanted. He also made sure his father knew nothing of his methods. Armando only revealed the result, another acquisition. Often, he would hire unsavory types to threaten owners, CEOs, and board members to comply with his demands. He didn't care what methods they used. He simply wanted the company he sought.

"Son, you've done so much in such a short time to grow our company. I feel it is in good hands and now I am ready to retire. I have more money than I can ever spend. I want to relax, play golf, and hang out with your mother."

Armando sat at the side table in his elaborate office. He had a southern exposure. So, from the 27th floor, he looked out of his floor-to-ceiling windows at Soldier Field, McCormick Place, the Planetarium, and Lake Michigan. On a clear, sunny day, the sun would shine for extended periods. As he listened to his dad, he focused on every word. His hands were tented with his fingertips touching each other. He was confident in his role as both son and the company's leader. Yet, he was purposeful in showing his father honor and respect. When his dad finished, he took a few seconds before responding. "Dad, you are my father and I love you. Thank you for having so much faith in me. I agree with whatever decision you want to make about retiring. You've earned it."

He watched his dad smile. It was clear to Armando his dad was happy and extremely content. He continued, "There is one more move I am going to make. If you are going to retire, I will wait until your transition is complete."

He watched his father's manner change.

His eyes narrowed, he moved forward to the edge of his chair, and he put his hands flat on the table. Then he said, "Son, what is this *one more move?*"

He immediately regretted having said anything. He looked down at the table, steadied himself, and then replied, "Look, Dad, we are a real force in our industry now. There is true respect for who we are and what we do. Our customers love us, and our competitors fear us. Nonetheless, we need one more acquisition to become the leader in our line of business."

He paid close attention to his father's reaction. He took notice of a new brightness in his eyes and the beginning of a smile on his face as he leaned back in his chair. He could almost see a question forming on his dad's lips.

"What acquisition are you talking about?"

Armando was prepared for the question. He, too, leaned back in his chair and said, "Universal…the acquisition is Universal Systems."

****

Armando chose to move to the South Loop. After some investigation, he selected a premier, luxury, full amenity building. His South Loop home located on the 43rd floor had everything he wanted. He had stunning views in every room, a northeast exposure, floor-to-ceiling windows, three bedrooms, three baths, three thousand square feet of space, a formal dining room, a kitchen with a spacious island, a theater pit which could seat up to fifteen people, and a building facility which housed a combined Olympic-size pool and a full workout center.

His parents wanted him to marry a nice Latina young lady, settle down, and have a house full of kids. His mother repeatedly said, "The business will always be there. Raising a family should be your priority."

But Armando was content to hold exclusive parties at his home, date different women with no commitments, and invest most of his time in building OMS. He felt he could marry and raise a family after he grew the company to be the biggest in the industry.

CHAPTER
FIFTEEN

CATHERINE HAD THOUGHT ABOUT NOTHING else but the conversation with Armando. She had rehearsed her lines multiple times. She went over everything she would be asked. So, from the back seat of this black Cadillac sedan, she continued looking at Armando Santos. She watched his expression, his eyes, and his forehead. He was a difficult man to read. Nevertheless, from their first meeting, she picked up small telltale signs on his face, and especially his eyes. She worked hard to keep her own voice evenly modulated. She made sure her facial expression conveyed a sense of confidence. So, as she began talking, she slightly raised her eyebrows and smiled.

"The plan is coming together. All the pieces are fitting together nicely. To this point, nothing has been left undone."

She watched him carefully. She could tell from his manner he was interested. He looked at her as she spoke without blinking. She noticed his pupils were more dilated than before she started talking about the elements of the plan. At the same time, his left hand covered his mouth to avoid the slight smile she barely noticed on his face.

He said, "Great! What's our next move?"

Catherine took her time answering. She quickly thought over her next sequence of remarks. Then she said, "As we planned, our guy on the board proposed Jack be made the permanent CEO. So, that's our next move."

She watched to see if he had a comment. When he didn't speak, she continued. "Jack's good friend and savior is now exactly where we want him. If the sexual harassment charges don't take him down, the offshore account definitely will."

Catherine could see Armando was formulating a question. Without taking his eyes off her, he said, "When the FBI finishes their investigation regarding where the money came from, where will the trail lead?"

Catherine anticipated the question. She knew he was not a man who asked a question without already knowing the answer. So, she played along; she leaned closer to him, put her hand on his shoulder and replied, "This is the best part. The trail will lead the FBI right to Jack Alexander's doorstep. He will be the CEO of Universal Systems who bribed an FBI Special Agent. When the dust settles, we will have taken them both down."

She stopped there to allow the impact of her words to sink in. She could see his eyes brighten. Now he didn't even try to hide the smile on his face. He said, "All right! That's what I'm talking about! The Universal stock will plummet and our bid to buy them will fly through with the help of our ally on the board of directors."

Catherine could see his eyes gleaming like she'd never seen before. Then he added, "We'll likely buy Universal for less than I originally planned. We both will have what we want. I'll have the last jewel in my company's portfolio, and you'll finally be able to bring down Jack Alexander. And he won't have Agent Harper as his little angel to come and save him."

The Cadillac sedan had driven north to the end of Lake Shore Drive, made its way back south, and was a few minutes from arriving at Catherine's hotel. Armando concluded, "You be certain nothing from here goes wrong."

Catherine hurriedly responded as the sedan slowed and was now a half block from the entrance to her hotel. "Nothing will go wrong."

He was quick to say, "It had better not."

Their eyes linked as Catherine grabbed the door handle and let herself out of the car.

CHAPTER
SIXTEEN

JACK SENT A TEXT TO Clarence.

We need to talk now. When can you call me?

From his house, he got in his car, backed out to the street, and drove away. He had only gone about a mile when his phone buzzed. Before he got on the expressway, he quickly pulled over and read:

Call you in five minutes.

Jack decided he would stay where he was and simply wait five minutes for Clarence to call him. His phone lit up and he answered it. "Clarence…how are you holding up, my friend?"

There was silence on the line. Finally, he heard, "Worse than when we last spoke. FBI agents showed up at my house with a warrant to search the premises. What they were looking for, I had no clue. Julie is still freaking out. She told me she is taking the kids and going to her mother's house until this whole thing gets sorted out. I can't blame her."

Jack waited to determine if he had more to say. When he heard nothing, he said, "Ouch. I have some more bad news."

He took a deep beath and continued, "I checked with our guy, and he won't be able to help beyond the sexual harassment charges. The only way he could find out anything about the bribery charges, he would have to hack into the FBI database. If he got caught, he'd be facing some serious prison time."

He held back to give him a chance to respond. After a protracted period of silence, Jack said, "Clarence, are you still there?"

"Yeah...what do you want me to say? I'm screwed and the Bureau is going to lock me up and throw away the key?"

Jack let him finish. Then he said, "You've never been one to cave in. During my hardest, most difficult times, you said to me, 'Jack, don't give up and don't give in.' Well, now I'm saying the same thing to you. Let's think about this differently. Our guy can't get the information we need. There must be another way. How can we find out more regarding the bribery charges against you? Who else can help us get what we need to know? Think, think...there has to be another way around this."

He waited to hear a response from Clarence. He heard nothing. He held the phone to his ear and closed his eyes. He put his left hand on his temple and started pressing on the chance some idea would pop out. When it seemed the situation was hopeless, he heard, "There is one thing I could try."

Jack eyes flew open. He was so surprised to hear his friend's voice. He blurted out, "What, what did you say?"

"I have an idea."

Jack was ecstatic. Things had progressed from hopeless to a possible idea. He said, "Okay, I'll bite, what's your idea?"

"Well, I could ask my boss for his help."

Jack was about to speak, but Clarence continued, "Harry has been my strongest advocate since I've been at the Bureau. If there is anyone I could trust, it would be him."

"Have you reached out to him since this whole thing happened?"

"No, honestly, with everything that's been going on, I didn't think about him until now."

"Hey, call him right now!"

Jack waited for him to speak. He figured he'd let everything sink in.

Clarence replied with, "I'll call him as soon as we hang up."

"Okay."

"All I can say is, thanks."

"No worries…keep me posted."

CHAPTER
SEVENTEEN

HARRY COOMBS, EXECUTIVE ASSISTANT Director of the CCRS (Criminal, Cyber, Response, and Service) branch, a member of the FBI for more than 30 years, his career spanned five presidents. For ages there was talk he would become the Director of the FBI. Harry was born in Alexandria, Virginia. His grandparents migrated from Kent, England and settled initially in New York in 1850. They eventually moved to the Washington, DC area. Harry's mother and father met, married, and raised their family in Alexandria.

He graduated from Harvard University and later earned a master's degree in International Relations from Georgetown University. After college, he joined the United States Marine Corp. where he served as an officer for four years in Vietnam. Among his commendations were both the Bronze Star and the Purple Heart. Following his military service, he earned a law degree from Harvard. When Clarence decided to join the FBI, Harry was one of the first people to evaluate and interview him. Harry was impressed with his background, his stated commitment to the Bureau, and his manner during their discussions.

Harry took him under his wing. Although Clarence reported to other people in the beginning, he kept a watchful eye over Clarence and monitored his progress. Eventually, Harry found a role which called for Clarence to report to him. So, Harry promoted him and continued to be his biggest supporter.

Clarence was clearly nervous when he finished the text and hit the Send arrow.

I think you know I'm in a jam right now. I need to have a short conversation with you. Where and when?

He sat in his car and waited. It was a bright, sunny day, but he was filled with gloom and turmoil. After ten minutes went by, he got a text.

Be at the Wendella boat dock by 11:30am.

Clarence starred at the message for a full minute and thought, *"Should I buy a ticket? Am I supposed to look for his car?"* Finally, he remembered something Harry constantly reminded him of: *'If I give you some instructions, don't read anything into them, just follow them to the letter.'*

****

He arrived at the boat dock at 11:20 a.m. He looked down at his cell phone for either a text or a phone call. The boat dock had a canopy over it and was below street level, so he couldn't see cars or people above him. He waited nervously. He watched the minutes tick away on his cell phone, 11:23, 11:25, 11:28. At 11:29 a.m., he looked up and saw Harry Coombs coming down the stairs to the dock. Harry looked every bit the FBI Director you'd anticipate seeing in a feature film. He was over six feet tall, clean-cut, strong Anglo features, strikingly attractive, stable hazel eyes that missed nothing. At fifty-five years old, he looked like a man in his early forties. He was dressed in a dark blue pin-stripe suit, a white well-laundered shirt, and a fashionable red tie.

Clarence watched as Harry walked over to him and put his hand on his shoulder.

"It's good to see you. How are you holding up?"

"Harry, thanks for coming."

"Come on, let's get on the boat."

Harry produced two tickets, handed them to the agent, and they boarded. They found a secluded spot and sat down as the boat left the dock. Clarence was the first to speak.

"It's pretty obvious I'm in a difficult situation. These charges against me are totally false. Sexual harassment...there must be some underlying reason why Agent Landers would bring such a baseless allegation. And to make matters worse, I get charged with supposedly taking bribes. You know I've never taken anything not belonging to me since I stepped into the Bureau."

He was about to continue when he realized Harry raised his hand to say something. He offered, "Look, I hear you. You have always been a stand-up guy and without question, I trust you. However, you need to answer a few questions."

"What?"

"How can you deny the bribery charges? They're so clear-cut, and the facts are hard to refute."

Clarence was taken aback by what he heard. He looked Harry straight in the eye and asked, "Facts like what?"

He realized he was asking Harry to share classified Bureau information. Nevertheless, at this point, he was running out of options. He took note of Harry's shifting posture. He placed his hands firmly on the little table separating them. After years of observing him, Clarence knew he was deciding what information, classified or not, he was going to share. Finally, he responded, "The bank account is clearly listed in your name. The basic information like social security number, home address, and driver's license were different like you were attempting to conceal your identity. True, we were given an anonymous tip. However, we wouldn't have known for sure, but there is a photo of you withdrawing funds."

He let him talk. Several times he wanted to stop him and scream, "I didn't have anything to do with this." But he held his tongue. He needed to hear as much as Harry was willing to share. Finally, he couldn't contain himself and he blurted out, "Where did the bribes come from?

As soon as he asked the question, he saw Harry get a strange look on his face. He squinted his eyes and he exhaled like he was trying to believe for himself what he was about to say. Clarence almost couldn't hear him as he spoke in a voice just above a whisper.

"That's the really weird part...the money trail leads back to your friend, Jack Alexander."

CHAPTER
EIGHTEEN

CATHERINE WALKED CONFIDENTLY THROUGH the hotel lobby. It had been a long time since she'd felt so self-assured. As she stepped into the elevator and pressed the button for the thirteenth floor, she marveled at how everything was falling into place. Again, she thought back to her introduction to Armando. Her contacts from prison convinced her Armando would be interested in her scheme if it fit his purposes. She did some investigation and determined his company's business model, as well as his acquisition strategy, was a match well suited for her. He wanted to acquire Universal, and she wanted to take down Jack. She could see early on her plan was of great interest to him. But he made it clear all plans would be completely under his control. Also, he let her know if anything went wrong, she would be left holding the bag. If the authorities ever started an investigation, he would disavow all knowledge of anything to do with their concocted game plan. He provided her with every needed resource, his people, tools, computer equipment, and money. Yet, she was obligated to keep him informed with every detail. Now the trap had been set and all the pieces were beginning to fall in place. She had a few more strings to pull and she would have *payback* in full. As she swiped the key to access her hotel room, her thoughts were on the calls she needed to make. She sat down at the hotel room's desk, opened her notebook, and pulled out her list of to-dos. When she had gone over it several times, she picked up her phone. The message she sent was direct.

Have everyone meet at our usual spot at 5pm. Make sure no one is late.

She waited for less than a minute and got a reply.

No worries…will meet you as previously planned.

****

Several days had passed since he'd learned of the crisis impacting Clarence and Len recovering from the car accident plus being dumped as CEO. Jack hadn't spent much time working in his new capacity. He decided to call a meeting of his senior leadership team. The team was the same as it had been prior to him becoming the interim CEO.

After his morning run, he showered, dressed, and came to the kitchen to spend a few minutes with Gloria before heading to the office.

"Hey, G, how are you this morning? It was late when I got home last night. I hope I didn't wake you."

Jack watched Gloria as she stood at the kitchen counter making breakfast. He still thought she was the most gorgeous woman he'd ever seen. She had such a radiant smile. Her glowing brown eyes sparkled. Remembering back to the time they were introduced; he couldn't take his eyes off her. She was five feet four, black hair with a sassy wave to it. She had a small waist and amazing curves in just the right places. Today, the outfit she'd selected fit her just right. He stood in the kitchen doorway, appreciating his lovely wife.

She finally said, "No, you didn't wake me. Come on in here, sit down, and eat something. Catch me up on what's going on with you, Clarence, Len, and your new role."

After Jack spent time explaining all the details, he realized he had to get to the office. But he noticed a strange look on Gloria's face. So, as he shoved the last piece of toast in his mouth, he asked her, "What's going on for you right now?"

She was quick to respond. "I'm concerned you are getting way too deep in this thing with Clarence and Len. I know how you feel about them both. Think about it, you don't work for the FBI. I don't want you to get yourself in trouble trying to help. This is an area where you have no experience at all."

"Look, babe, your concerns are real, and I have more to say. However, I've got to run. I'll fill you in on some more details later tonight. I love you."

"I love you too. But please give some thought to what I said. Have a great day."

NINETEEN

THE SENIOR LEADERS WERE ALL on time, eight o'clock sharp. Jack made a brief announcement regarding Len's condition. He didn't feel the need to spend a lot of time on it because the formal announcement with all the details had already been made. He wanted to make sure all members of the team were pulling their weight and fulfilling their respective roles. He knew it would be critical for all their employees, clients, and industry analysts to feel Universal Systems was in good hands.

The meeting went according to plan. While a few issues came up, they were small and very manageable. Jack received each business unit's management report and he applauded them for their progress. He also made sure not to reference anything about him becoming the permanent CEO. He did make mention to the new fiscal year's plan and thanked them for their contributions.

As the meeting adjourned, Matthew Warren, the new CFO, asked if he could spend a few minutes talking to him. Matthew was hired to replace Toni Lucas, the CFO who was involved in the kidnapping plot. She, unfortunately, lost her life before she'd been convicted for her part in the conspiracy. Universal took time interviewing multiple candidates before hiring Matthew. He proved to be an excellent hire and had taken the CFO role to a new level. Jack was especially pleased to have a strong person of integrity.

As the two of them walked to Jack's office, he said, "Matthew, how long has it been since you came to us, eighteen months?"

"Yes, just about that. "

"Well, all of your peers have only tremendous things to say about you."

When they got to his office, Jack told him to go in and sit down. He then took a few minutes to catch up with messages and any sensitive issues his executive assistant had for him. Once he finished, he walked into his office, closed the door, and sat down.

"So, Matthew, what is it you wanted to talk to me about?"

He noticed him looking down at his notes before responding. Clearly, this was important because he was making sure he got it right. Then he looked up and said, "I got a call from a Roger Underwood. He is a Special Agent from the Department of Justice."

Jack's eyebrows went up as he was surprised by the comment. He didn't respond, hoping Matthew had more to add.

He continued, "When I asked the nature of the call, he said he was from the Criminal Division, specifically the Fraud section."

Jack moved slightly forward in his chair. "The Criminal division…the Fraud section? What did he want?"

"He requested a meeting. He said he had a series of questions he wanted to ask me. I didn't feel comfortable with simply granting him a meeting time without talking to you first."

Now Jack was uncomfortable. He moved around in his chair, started rubbing his hands together under his desk, and looked down for a few seconds. He tried to remain calm, but he was shaken by Matthew's comments. His mind immediately went back to Gloria's words. *"I'm concerned you are getting way too deep in this thing with Clarence."* He asked himself, *"Is this about Clarence or something else? Why would the Department of Justice be coming here to Universal? I can't ignore this request. I must find out exactly what they want."*

Matthew interrupted his thoughts. "What do you want me to do? What would you like me to say?"

Jack looked down at his hands which were planted flat on his desk. Finally, he answered in a voice just above a whisper. "Call him back and tell him we will meet with him. Check with my assistant to find an acceptable day and time."

Then he added, "Also, get in touch with Tom Wallace, our general counsel. I want to make sure he is with us at this meeting. Keep me posted if there are any additional developments."

"Anything else?"

He considered the question before saying, "No, no, that's all. And Matthew, thanks for checking with me…appreciate it."

"Absolutely!"

Matthew got up and headed for the door. Just before he opened it, he turned and said, "Is there anything for us to worry about?"

Jack slowly looked up from his desk. His wrinkled brow told a different story than his words. "No, no, we'll be fine."

With that, Matthew opened the door, walked out, and closed it behind him.

Jack was left alone with his thoughts. *"This entire situation is getting a bit crazy. If the Department of Justice is coming here, I'm sure it's not a social call. I feel ill-equipped to handle this. Normally, I would call either Len or Clarence. Given their respective situations, it wouldn't be appropriate to drag them into this one. After all, it could be nothing, a false alarm. But why does everything in me suggest this is a big deal? I need help and I'm not sure where to turn. Maybe calling Len is a good idea. He will likely have some perspective for me. Plus, I need to share with him the accident report."*

CHAPTER
TWENTY

JACK FINISHED HIS TEXT TO Len.

> **I need to talk to you. It's important. Let me know when you are available.**

He only had to wait for a couple of minutes for a reply.

> **I will call you in ten minutes. Thanks.**

When his cell phone rang, he picked up the call. "Len, thanks for calling back."

"Right. What's up? What did you find out about the accident?"

Jack told him what he found out about the car, the call from the Justice Department, and his efforts to help Clarence.

Len responded, "For different reasons, these situations are problematic. What your contact found out about the car makes it crystal clear someone was, and probably still is, interested in taking me out permanently. Regarding the Justice Department's upcoming visit, I'm not sure what it means. You'll have to wait and see. Nevertheless, I think it's wise to have Tom Wallace sit in on the meeting. He's a smart lawyer and will know how to handle things."

"You and your wife might be vulnerable at home."

There was an extended pause on the line. He could tell Len was thinking and pondering his next comment. Finally, he heard, "I believe the intent was to get me out of Universal. Their mission was accomplished. For what, I don't know."

****

"You understand this is simply a preliminary investigation. We only need to ask a few questions."

Jack sat with his CFO and General Counsel at their conference room table. They were staring at three people from the Justice Department and two people from the FBI. The lead for this meeting was Ralph Martinez, Assistant Director from the Justice Department's Criminal division. He was forty-five years old, five feet nine, and had the signs of a previously broken nose from his early years in the Golden Gloves. Growing up in a Puerto Rican neighborhood in Brooklyn meant he was repeatedly challenged on his way to and from school. His dad took him to a gym to learn boxing so he could defend himself. He excelled and made the Golden Gloves team. In his semi-final bout for the regional championships, he stepped into a left hook from his opponent who fractured his nose in three places. He decided it was time to give up the sport and focus on college. At NYU, he earned his undergraduate degree. Later, he applied to Yale Law school and was accepted. After a military stint with the Navy, he joined the Justice Department. He moved rapidly through the ranks. He was named to the role of Assistant Director in the Justice department's Criminal division. His ultimate objective was to be nominated by the next

President as Attorney General and become a member of the Presidential cabinet. When this case came across his desk, he saw it as an opportunity to add another feather in his cap. At the same time, he needed to make sure all went according to plan. He knew Jack Alexander was a high-flyer. He read all the background on him and his relationship with Clarence Harper. He had told his team in the days leading up to the meeting, "Let me do the talking. If I need anything from you folks, I will ask you. I want you to be my 'optical muscle.' If there is something here, we will root it out."

Jack had been told by his General Counsel to remain silent unless he asked him a question. Jack was also told the range of answers he should respond with. When Tom started off the meeting, Jack was observing everyone in the room.

"So, Mr. Martinez, since your department requested this meeting, how can we help you?"

Jack watched as Martinez appeared to be going over his notes before he spoke. Yet, it was clear he knew exactly what he'd plan to cover.

"Are you Jack Alexander?"

Jack almost laughed out loud. This guy knew who the CEO was long before he walked into the building. Nonetheless, Tom said, "No, I am Tom Wallace, General Counsel here at Universal Systems. Again, how can we help you?"

"Well, I would like to ask your CEO some questions."

Tom spoke up again. "Yes, while I understand, please tell me the nature of your questions and we will try to accommodate them."

"Okay, how long has Mr. Alexander been here at Universal Systems? Where did he come from and who hired him?"

After Tom answered the Assistant Director's questions, Jack sat back and watched as the group took notes in silence. Again, he was reasonably certain they knew these answers before they came. Martinez looked up from his notes and asked, "How does Mr. Alexander know Special Agent Clarence Harper of the FBI and what is their relationship?"

Jack could tell Tom wasn't totally prepared for this question but to his credit, he never missed a beat. He said, "Why is this important?"

"We are simply trying to get some answers to some basic questions. We can do this here or we can subpoena Mr. Alexander and ask these same questions in open court. I'm sure the press would love it."

Jack could see Tom was getting riled by Martinez's cavalier attitude. Jack didn't want to usurp Tom's responsibility as General Counsel, but it appeared things were about to take a bad turn. He decided to hold his tongue and keep quiet. Tom then said in an even tone, "I would simply like to know the purpose of your questions."

"Mr. Wallace, these are just questions helping us to understand a few things."

"Like what?"

"Please just answer our questions."

Jack observed Tom as he leaned back in his chair and proceeded to provide Martinez with what he asked for. He could see Martinez write down a few things, review his notes, and then look up at Tom and Jack before he said, "Would you be surprised if I told you Agent Harper was under investigation for taking bribes?"

Tom, Jack, and Matthew were quiet for an extended period. Finally, Tom spoke, "I don't know Agent Harper well enough to answer your question. However, from the little I do know about him, I would consider him to be loyal and honest in his profession."

"What about you, Mr. Alexander? Would you be surprised?"

He was about to answer when Tom spoke. "Mr. Martinez, please direct all of your questions to me. You asked and I answered your question. I've instructed Mr. Alexander to let me answer for both him and our firm. So, is there anything else?"

Jack followed Martinez's movements as he sat forward in his chair. His eyes narrowed and he started clenching his teeth. He looked straight at Tom without blinking his eyes and said, "Mr. Wallace, I'll ask the questions here."

Jack could tell Martinez was getting really riled up. He watched him smile broadly, consciously sit back in his chair, put his pen down, and say, "Sorry, I was a bit harsh. So, let's start again. How often does Agent Harper visit you folks here at Universal? How long has he held Universal stock? Who would he visit whenever he came here?"

Jack could see how the other people who came with Martinez took an interest in these questions. They now sat poised in front of their iPad or with a pen above their respective notebooks. But Tom never lost his cool. He casually said, "Agent Harper has never been a regular visitor here, not since years ago when our CEO was kidnapped. Also, I am not aware of Agent Harper ever being a shareholder. As you know, since Universal Systems is a publicly traded stock, anyone who buys our stock would be a shareholder. Also, unless the shares were sizeable, we wouldn't know who held them. Lastly, it is common knowledge Agent Harper and our CEO have known each other since college. So, if Agent Harper did come here, Mr. Alexander would likely be the person he would come to see."

The next question shocked Jack and his two colleagues. "Would it surprise you if I told you Agent Harper is under investigation for taking bribe money which has been tracked back to your CEO, Mr. Jack Alexander?"

He was stunned by what he'd just heard. Of all the things he'd anticipated, this was not one of them. He thought to himself, *"How could this be possible? Bribery…this is so far from the truth. I haven't ever done a dishonest thing since I've been in business, and certainly not at Universal."* He looked over at Tom who remained steady as a rock. He never blinked or looked flustered. As he looked at Martinez, he was calm and collected, his hands were steady, and his manner didn't deviate. He smoothly stated, "Our CEO is an honest, upstanding man. Bribery is not in his DNA. You must be mistaken."

Martinez stayed with his line of questioning, "You are saying Mr. Alexander has not ever bribed Agent Harper?"

"If you have any evidence to the contrary, we are asking you to produce it."

With this comment, Martinez backtracked slightly. "Look, we don't want to jump to unfair conclusions. We'd like your CFO to provide us with a list of certain transactions and whose name is associated with them. Also, we'd like Mr. Alexander to provide us access to his personal bank accounts over a certain period. If these things check out, we will withdraw our claim. If not, we will likely prosecute your CEO and possibly others in your firm."

There was a long, protracted period when no one said anything, and the two sides simply looked at each other. Finally, Tom spoke. "We have nothing to hide. Send an email with your request and we will provide you with our response."

He saw Tom take out his business card and slide it slowly across the table in Martinez's direction. Then he added, "Send your request to the email address on my card. If there is nothing further, I believe this meeting is over."

Jack watched Martinez pick up Tom's card, quickly look at it, put it in his shirt pocket, close his notebook, and stand. He said, "Fine, we will get our requests over to you within the week."

He extended his hand to Tom and shook it and did the same with Matthew. He then shook Jack's hand but held on to it for an extended period. Jack absorbed the man's stare. Martinez said, "In my opinion, you are in trouble, my friend."

Jack said nothing but stayed focused on Martinez and the rest of the group as they filed out of the conference room. Martinez was the last one to reach the door. Before he walked out, he turned and said, "Oh, one more thing, what's your time commitment to get your response back to us?"

Tom was quick to reply. "I can't answer that without seeing your request. So, let's leave it there for now."

With that, Martinez turned and walked out.

TWENTY-ONE

"**O**KAY PEOPLE, LET'S GO OVER the items we still need to put in place. We are quickly approaching the final phase and there can't be any slip-ups."

Catherine was standing in front of the team responsible for creating all the havoc for Len Shapiro, Clarence Harper, and especially Jack Alexander. Armando had kept his word by giving her his best people to carry out this elaborate plan. He'd trusted her to make it all happen.

She continued. "Frank, you provided the anonymous tips to the FBI regarding the bribery monies in Agent Harper's account, where it came from, and the photos of him making withdrawals. Sophia, you worked it out so Agent Landers would allege that Agent Harper had sexually assaulted her. She believes we won't distribute the video of her brother giving drugs to a minor and then watching her OD. Harold, your guys crippled Len Shapiro's car to take him out as CEO at Universal. Carlos, your threat to Shane McCarthy, the board chairman at Universal worked. He is doing everything we need on the inside. He convinced the rest of the board to replace Lenard Shapiro with Jack Alexander. He also got them to strongly consider making Alexander the permanent CEO."

Catherine took a minute and looked around the room at each person. She was reveling in the reality of Jack Alexander's imminent downfall. She knew all the final puzzle pieces she needed to put in place. "Now we are going to move ahead and put the bow on the package. We've already heard from our sources at the FBI and the Justice department. They have started an investigation into the bribery charges. This will go a long way in achieving our final plan. Now, Frank, I need you to use your sources at the two news agencies to leak this story. Remember, use the exact wording, 'From confirmed sources.' Sophia, make sure Agent Landers uses our strongly recommended language during the FBI internal hearing. Remind her again what's at stake. Carlos, now you need to lay out for Shane McCarthy, the board chairman, exactly what he needs to do next. He must communicate his shock to the other board members about the bribery charges, arrange for a press conference to express his surprise and worry, and make sure he contacts the selected financial institutions to confidentially voice his lack of confidence in the company and its stock. Thomas, you need to get your people to start dropping hints about the CEO's bribery charges to the largest clients of Universal. Oh, one more thing, Carlos, McCarthy needs to suggest to the board they should put Alexander on administrative leave until the federal investigation is over. Also, they should make McCarthy the acting CEO for continuity sake."

Catherine waited to determine if there were any questions. As she looked from one face to the next, she only saw heads nodding. She felt like everyone was on board with her plan. She added, "Since there are no questions, let's get going as our scheduled implementation time is critical. Also, only use the burner cellphones I gave you, and only call me with either updates or if you have a problem. Okay, this meeting is over."

****

Jack was stunned by the meeting with the Justice department and the FBI. What he heard regarding the bribery allegations had his head spinning. After the Feds left, he watched Tom fall back in his chair. Jack looked over at Matthew who was silent and doodling in his notebook.

Tom was the first to speak. "We need to debrief what just happened."

"Sure, sure...Matthew, I'll be interested in your thinking as well."

Jack collected his thoughts and said, "First, Tom, you did an amazing job handling the meeting with all of its nuances. You both likely have a dozen questions. Yet, at the top of the list is probably the bribery allegation. Let me assure you, I have never bribed anyone, and certainly not Agent Harper. I owe the guy my life, but I would never compromise his career or mine by doing anything so stupid."

He stopped and waited for a reaction from either Tom or Matthew. Tom turned and looked Jack squarely in the face. He could see Tom's manner was mild and non-threatening. He saw a softness in his eyes and a slight smile on his face as he said, "I've watched you all these years here at the company. If there is one thing I know, you are a man of integrity. You see, I believe the definition of integrity is what you do when no one is looking. Len has always trusted you and so have I."

He stopped. Jack could tell he had more to say, so he waited. Tom did not disappoint. "Where did these allegations come from? Eleven million dollars, that's crazy. I don't understand."

"Well, for sure, this has to be someone trying to put me and Universal in a bad light. The questions for me are who and why?"

Jack looked over at Matthew who was simply sitting and listening. He said, "This must be a lot for you to take in. You've been quiet through this whole thing. What's on your mind?"

He could see Matthew was struggling to formulate his thoughts into words. Eventually, he spoke. "I've been sitting here trying to determine what the specific requests will be from the Feds and how will we respond. Honestly, I've never been involved in anything like this in the past."

Tom responded by saying, "Matthew if it's any comfort, neither have we. This is all new territory. The reason why I told them to put their requests in writing was so we could have some react time. Jack, if it is all right with you, I will call some legal confidantes of mine and get some professional opinions."

"Great idea. In the meantime, I want you two to keep this strictly confidential. Is that understood?"

He saw them both nod their heads and then say almost in unison, "Of course, we won't say a word unless you say so."

"Guys, thank you for your confidence in me and your involvement. Tom, let me know as soon as you find out something."

****

Jack walked back to his office. His mind was filled with thoughts and questions. He was having a difficult time sorting through everything. He walked right by his executive assistant, went into his office, and closed the door. He sat down at his desk, leaned back, and covered his eyes with his hands. A couple minutes passed, and he heard a knock on his door. He sat up and responded, "Yes, who is it?"

Beth, his executive assistant, stood at the door. She said, "Can I come in?"

"Yes, yes, come on in, take a seat. What's going on?"

He could see Beth's hesitancy. She looked down at her hands in her lap for a few seconds. Then she looked up at Jack. She said, "I have known you for years. I have watched you perform under several different scenarios. We have worked together, and you have always been honest with me. I can tell these last few weeks have been extremely stressful for you, but you have not shared anything with me. I sense I would be a greater support if I knew what you were experiencing. You are under no obligation to confide in me, but that would be different than how you have done things in the past. Sharing whatever is going on may not help you, but it would allow me to be a better assistant and friend to you."

He was surprised by what Beth said. He thought she was coming in to discuss some business-related topic. It did cause him to reflect on his relationship with her.

When he first came to Universal, Beth was assigned to him as his assistant. Since he was new to the company, he relied heavily on her for virtually everything. Beth had been at the company for three years prior and had worked for two different vice-presidents. She knew her way around. Before Jack started, Len invited her into his office. "Beth, you have been with us long enough to know how things run around here. Your last two managers had nothing but good things to say about you. How are you enjoying your time here?"

Beth was surprised at being in the CEO's office. She'd had only one other brief conversation with him in the three years she'd worked at Universal. So, this was highly unusual for her. She thought about his question and said, "Mr. Shapiro, I have really appreciated my time here at the company. It has been a rewarding experience and I have learned a lot. My managers have treated me fairly and they have been pleased with the value I've provided."

"Good, I'm glad. I have a new challenge for you. We just hired a guy who will be starting in a few weeks. He is talented in many areas, but he has never worked for us. I need someone to be his assistant who knows what happens here and can provide high value. When I asked the other leaders, they told me you would be the best person for this assignment."

Beth was surprised. She expressed her satisfaction. "Thank you, Mr. Shapiro, for your confidence in me. I look forward to taking on this new opportunity."

As she left the CEO's office, she reflected on her career. After high school, she went to work in a bank as a teller. It didn't pay enough for her to move out and get her own apartment. So, she started looking for another job on her off days. There was a big company in the downtown Loop called Universal Systems. They needed someone to work in their administrative area being an assistant to multiple managers. She excelled in the role, and she was made an assistant to a director who gave her lots of increased responsibilities. She was a quick study and the director started giving her special projects to complete.

After some time passed, the director left the company. He had provided his excellent reviews to management regarding Beth's capabilities. She was made an executive assistant for a vice-president and the rest was history.

The conversation and offer from Len provided her with more money. She liked Jack and they worked well together. He relied on her and regularly took her into his confidence. So, when the recent events happened, Beth was surprised when he didn't confide in her.

Jack looked at Beth as she now sat in front of him. She had shared her thoughts and waited for him to respond. He said, "Beth, I am sorry for not talking to you specifically about the changes happening around here. It was an oversight for me to shut you out. Please accept my apology. You continue to be an asset to me, and nothing has changed. What would you like to know?"

"Well, first of all, what's really going on?"

Jack spent the next thirty minutes giving her the essential items associated with the recent events. It turned out, some of them she knew, but most of them she had no clue. At the end of his comments, he said, "I know this goes without saying, but none of what I have shared with you is repeatable."

"As always…my lips are sealed."

"Thanks for coming in and taking a risk to talk to me about all this. It makes me appreciate even more your importance to me."

"Well, I know you have a bunch to finish before you leave here, and so do I. Thanks again."

Beth got up, turned, open the door, walked out, and closed it softly.

CHAPTER
TWENTY-TWO

JACK'S THOUGHTS WENT FROM THE conversation with Beth to the immediacy of the situation before him. Several more minutes went by as he pondered all he heard in the meeting with the Feds. He thought, *"Federal agents, an investigation, Len's accident, Clarence, sexual harassment, bribery charges...Lord, what in the world is going on?"* His phone buzzed, letting him know he had a text message. He almost ignored it. But he picked it up, looked at the message, and realized it was from Clarence.

We need to talk! Call me ASAP. How soon can you call me?

He sat looking at the message. With all that was going on, he needed a little time to process it. He got up and headed out of his office. He told Beth to cancel and reschedule all his calls and appointments for the next two hours. The elevator was empty, and he was again alone in his thoughts. As he pushed open the door to the street, he immediately felt the warm summer breeze. He headed south along Michigan Avenue. Once he reached Madison Avenue, he crossed the street and headed east toward Grant Park. He crossed over the old train yard and when he reached Columbus Drive, he again started walking south. Jack didn't have a destination in mind. He wandered along, looking at the new wing of the Art Institute, Buckingham Fountain, and the Petrillo band shell. It was a nice sunny day. The wind blew slightly from the east, away from Lake Michigan. He walked for an indefinite period. Finally, he sat down on a park bench. He started noticing the bike riders, the runners, and the people walking and talking to each other. He observed their smiling faces as they appeared to be sharing pleasantries with each other. Some were holding hands, while others walk along slowly in a constant side-to-side hug.

His mind shifted to the multiple issues plaguing him. He was finding it increasingly difficult to know what to do, what steps to take, or how to help anyone, including himself. Jack sat there, closed his eyes, and said a prayer. *"Father, you promised never to leave me nor forsake me. With all I am facing; I need your help and guidance now more than ever. I'm not sure what to do right now. Your direction would be a beautiful thing right now. Thanks in advance."*

He slowly opened his eyes, not exactly sure what to expect. But no one walked up to him with a message. And he didn't see any words written in the sky. Yet, he did notice a sense of peace and calm. In addition, he did get a strong urge to call Clarence. He took out his phone and sent a message.

> **Sorry it has taken me a long time to respond to you. I can call you now.**

He got an immediate text.

> **Yes, please do.**

Jack punched his number into his burner phone.

Clarence answered on the first ring. "Hey, man, when you didn't text me back, I started to worry. What's going on with you?"

He took the time to explain the meeting with the Feds and his findings regarding Len's car. Then he listened as Clarence laid out the meeting with his boss, Harry. When he finished, Jack said, "So, it seems you and I are in a really bad situation. Basically, what is Harry's recommendation for a plan going forward?"

Clarence continued, "Harry told me he is going to conduct his own personal investigation into this. What he is going to do is completely off the record and dangerous for him. If someone finds out, he could be in big trouble. When I thanked him, he looked me in the eye and said, 'Clarence, you're worth it.'"

The two of them talked for a while longer. They talked about how all of this was impacting their families. Clarence asked about the potential aftereffects Jack could likely experience at Universal. Before they hung up, they discussed next steps with each other.

"I still have our guy looking into some things. I will circle back with you when I have something. When did Harry say he would get back to you?"

"I'll hear from him as soon as he has anything."

****

Jack walked back to his office building and rode the elevator up to his floor. He spent the next two hours taking his scheduled calls and meetings. Afterwards, he made some notes associated with things he needed to follow up on before leaving the office. On the ride home, he called Fred Russell since he hadn't heard from him.

Fred took a while before he answered. "Hey, I'm sorry for the delay. It's taken a minute for me to dig into this without it blowing back on me."

"So, what have you found that's useful? The noose around our friend's neck is getting tighter with each passing day."

Jack didn't hear Fred reply. All he heard was the sound of rustling paper. Eventually Fred said, "Yeah, I did uncover some stuff I believe will be helpful. It turns out Agent Landers has a brother who's been on the 'dark side' for years. He's a drug user and a two-bit pusher. He's got a rap sheet with a lot of activity on it. While he has served some time, it has never been for anything serious. His sister, Agent Landers, has tried to get him help, but it hasn't worked. A narcotics police detective in Alexandria, Virginia, a friend of mine, told me something major happened involving Bobby, her brother. He didn't know exactly what it was, but it was significant enough to get Agent Landers to come to Alexandria over it. The only thing I can tell you is she came, she had a couple of meetings, and the whole thing went away before it ever saw the light of day."

Jack thought for a minute as he looked at the expressway in front of him. Then he asked, "What do you think it was?"

"Must be something big enough to cause her to allege sexual harassment on our guy."

"That's nuts. It makes no sense."

"All I can tell you is the timeline. Agent Landers goes to Alexandria, spends two days, and goes back to Chicago. The next day, the issue with her brother disappears and the same day Agent Landers files a sexual harassment charge against our guy. The two events are too linked to be simply coincidence."

He thought more about what he'd just heard. He was snapped back from his thoughts when Fred said, "Jack, are you still there?"

"Yeah, so…someone put pressure on her to make this bogus claim. Is there anything else you can find out without compromising yourself?"

"I've gone as far as I can go without bringing heat down on me."

"I get it. Thanks for your help. If you find out anything else, be sure to let me know right away."

"I wish I could do more."

CHAPTER
TWENTY-THREE

RACHEL FRAZIER CHECKED THE WEATHER app on her phone. Since it indicated the weather would be perfect all day, she decided not to take her umbrella on her way to school. She walked down State Street and made her way over to Michigan Avenue. As she went along, she reflected on her three years in Chicago and her tenure at the Art Institute. She'd learned so much about the city and had come to appreciate it a lot more than her growing-up years in Atlanta. Her father had repeatedly asked her to consider coming back home once she graduated. But Rachel was convinced Chicago would be her home city, at least for the foreseeable future. As a result of school, she had built a 'friend' community and she felt she was thriving. She regretted her breakup with her old boyfriend Luke. He was the one who originally suggested she apply to the Art Institute. He had come to Chicago before she did. She had strong feelings for him. However, they realized after her first year in the city, they had interests taking them in different directions. Also, after her mom was released from Federal prison and had come to live with her, Rachel wanted to distance herself from anything and anyone reminding her of the events involving the kidnapping she'd witnessed of Jack Alexander. She had stayed away from her mother as well. Rachel told her mother she would need to move out and find a place of her own. Now, almost three years had passed, and she still anguished over the decision. She sent her mother birthday and Mother's Day cards, but she hadn't seen her since she moved out.

Her artwork was her life now. She excelled in her classes, and she was developing her own style. Abstract art was her passion. Her instructors encouraged her, and she had been featured in numerous shows. She was thrilled with her progress, and she believed this would be her life's work. Her artistic advisor had linked her up with some galleries for the purpose of displaying her work. She was establishing a following, she'd sold a few pieces, and she'd been interviewed for the Art Section in two Chicago magazines. She'd had help, but she'd created a website as a vehicle to promote her brand, build a reputation, and sell more of her work.

She did have some remorse. While her dad had seen her work, come to her gallery showings, and had applauded her success, Rachel wanted to get approval from her mother. This had been the case since she was a little girl. For hours, she would sit on the floor quietly while her mother conducted phone meetings. Rachel loved to show off her schoolwork to her mother in between her conference calls. When her mother went to prison, Rachel suffered greatly. But now, all those things had passed. She almost called her mother to come to one of her art showings. But she realized before she completed the call, opening that door would be a mistake.

The walk to school was enjoyable and relaxing. The sun was shining, and it seemed everyone she passed was happy and smiling. She was so caught up in her thoughts, the mile walk went by quickly. As she walked to the building, she started reflecting on the events of her day, and it made her smile.

****

Catherine took another sip of her espresso; it tasted great. As she put it down, she continued to look over the long list of items she needed to ensure got completed. She knew Armando would not tolerate any mistakes. What needed to come together over the next few days was critically important; there could be no slip-ups.

****

Armando picked up his phone and used his speed dial to reach Javier Moreno. Moreno was head of Mergers and Acquisitions for OMS Corporation.

Javier picked up on the first ring. "Mr. Santos, what can I do for you?"

He wasted no time in responding. "Everything set for your call to Universal Systems?"

"Yes, sir, everything is right on schedule. "

"Fine, fine, let's now move forward with the next steps."

"Okay, I will personally make the call to Universal today, letting them know we are interested in immediately acquiring them."

"Make sure you let them know we would like a meeting asap. As soon as you get a reaction, let me know."

"Absolutely."

"I'll be waiting."

Instantly, he hung up, leaned back in his chair, and tented his fingers. With every other acquisition, he had been confident of his desired outcome. Since this one was larger than any other, he continued to weigh every aspect of his plan carefully.

CHAPTER
TWENTY-FOUR

JACK WAS DRIVING INTO THE office when his cell phone buzzed. He looked and saw the incoming call was from Tom Wallace. He picked up.

"Tom, how are you today?"

"How long before you get into the office?"

"About fifteen minutes, why? What's up?"

"I just got the email from the Feds. I need to go over the items they are requesting."

"Okay, what are they?"

"Not now, I can wait until you get here. Have Beth call me, and I can walk over."

"Anything else?"

"Well, since you mentioned it, I got an M and A call from a company interested in acquiring Universal."

"We'll cover that when I see you. "

"You bet."

Jack hit the End button, looked out on Lake Michigan for an instant, and thought about the start of his day. *"FBI requests, a call to buy our company, and a host of other issues."*

****

Jack and Beth spent thirty minutes going over his schedule for the day. As they were coming to the end of their meeting, she remarked, "A reporter from the *Chicago Tribune* called wanting to talk to you. He essentially wanted you to confirm or deny you are being investigated by the FBI on bribery charges."

Jack was leaning over his desk reviewing his schedule. When he heard what Beth said, he sat straight back in his chair and stared at her with the most perplexing look on his face. "What did you say?"

"I said, a reporter called you wanting to know—"

"I heard what you said, what did you tell him?"

"I said, you were not in, and he would have to call back."

He sat there in shock for several seconds without moving. His eyes were focused blankly on the wall in front of him. Then his mouth started twisting and his right hand shook.

Beth said, "Mr. Alexander, are you alright? Should I call someone because you don't look well right now."

Beth's words caused him to snap out of what was going on for him. He answered in something just above a whisper, "I'm okay...I'm all right."

112

Beth said slowly, "Okay…What should I tell the reporter? He said he would be calling back."

Jack was equally slow to respond. "Beth…if he calls back, tell him Universal has no comment."

"Yes, but he said they were going to print this story."

He responded more quickly, "When he calls back, simply tell him Universal has no comment. Now if you have nothing else for me, please let Tom Wallace know I am ready to meet with him. Thanks, Beth."

With that, he watched Beth collect her notes and leave his office. Jack was left alone with his thoughts. *"The* Chicago Tribune, *how did they know about this? Who would have told them? Are there other news agencies that know about this? What about the financial institutions? This could have a real negative impact on our stock price and the image of the company."*

His desk phone rang. He picked it up,

"Mr. Wallace is here to see you."

"Send him in. Thanks, Beth."

Tom opened the door, walked in, and sat down.

Jack saw his furrowed brow and knew Tom was troubled. "Tom, let's talk about the Feds' request. What exactly do they want?"

"I think we have bigger issues right now."

"Really? Like what?"

"Yesterday, I received a call from a Javier Moreno. He is the head of Mergers and Acquisitions for OMS Corporation. You may not be aware of them, but their business model is like ours except they are a smaller player."

"So, what's the issue?"

"He called and indicated his firm wants to buy Universal. When I told him we are likely not interested, he proceeded to tell me we should seriously consider what they have to offer."

"And you said...?"

"I told him what you have communicated to the senior leadership team...'You can't refuse something you know nothing about.' When I told him that, he began to tell me they wanted to move quickly."

"And?"

"I told him to email me whatever he had, and we would get back to him."

Jack took a few reflective seconds before responding. Then he said, "So, what's the big deal? We have others who have been interested in acquiring us. Why is this so troubling to you?"

"I hung up talking to him and the very next call was from the *Chicago Sun-Times*."

Now, for the second time, he sat ramrod straight in his chair, looked at Tom, and said, "What? What did they want?"

"First of all, it was a woman reporter. She said they had plans on running a lead story about the CEO of Universal being investigated by the FBI and the Justice Department on alleged bribery charges. She asked, 'Before we run the story, we want to find out if there is any truth to what we were told.'"

"What did you tell her?"

"I simply said we have no comment." He was still pensive. Nonetheless, he tried to relax.

Then Tom added, "To me, it's more than coincidental receiving those two calls back-to-back. Plus, why would those calls come to me? In all the years of being here, I have never received an M and A call or a call from the media. Something seems off here and I don't know exactly what it is."

"What you don't know is Beth received a call from the *Tribune* asking basically the same thing. By the way, what did the Feds request in their email?"

He watched Tom open his file and pull out a document. "Detailed information on you, the company, accounts, transactions, and any financial records we have regarding Agent Harper. Also, they have a fairly aggressive timeline as to when the request needs to be responded to."

"Can we get it all together and get back to them or do we need to ask for an extension?"

"The Feds don't like to give extensions. I also don't want them to think we are trying to hide anything."

Jack looked at the list and then handed it back to Tom. "Is this everything they want?"

"I'm more concerned about the acquisition call and the media issue. What would you like me to do about either of them?"

"First, there is nothing we can do about the story. It is what it is. But once you get any details from OMS, let me know immediately."

Jack could tell Tom had more he wanted to say. "What's bugging you?"

"Something is going on here that's not quite clear yet. It has me more than mildly concerned. While I can't put my finger on it, my radar is definitely engaged."

Jack leaned back, put his elbows on the side of his chair, and took a deep breath. Then he asked, "You think someone is behind all this. You're sensing a plot of some kind?"

"I don't have an answer, but for sure, something isn't right."

They sat in silence for a few seconds. With conviction, he offered, "Let's leave it right there. You need to get with Matthew and complete the Feds' request. If anything else happens, or if you have anything more concrete, call me on my cell."

"I will."

He stood and Tom followed suit. They shook hands and Jack added, "Tom, thanks for all your help and for taking the lead of this."

"No worries…happy to."

With that said, Jack watched Tom turn and walk to the door. Before he left, he said, "A word to the wise…watch your back."

It took him a few seconds to consider the weight of Tom's comment. Yet, he knew Tom was right. There were too many things running together. Tom made the statement without knowing the whole story.

CHAPTER
TWENTY-FIVE

JACK TRIED TO DISTRACT HIMSELF by looking at his schedule for the rest of the day. He wanted to cancel everything and head home. But he knew he couldn't do that. Instead, he put his head down and powered through the day. Before he realized it, 8:00 p.m. had arrived and he was still sitting at his desk. He began packing up to leave when his cell phone started buzzing. He looked to see who was calling. It was Shane McCarthy. He wanted to let the call go to voicemail, but he decided to take it.

"Hello, Shane."

"What is this business about you being investigated by the Feds on bribery charges?"

He took a deep breath and responded, "What you heard is true. The Feds have opened an investigation, erroneously. They are looking into whether I have anything to do with bribing a federal agent."

He waited to determine if he would get a response. It didn't take long.

"This is unconscionable. How could anything like this be happening? I hope you have thought about how this will impact the image of the company. We're in real trouble here."

He thought Shane was waiting for a reply, but he was simply talking a pause to catch his breath. "And to think we are days away from making you permanent CEO. I had to reach out to you to make sure this accusation was accurate. I've called an emergency board meeting for tomorrow afternoon. I strongly suggest you be present at the meeting to explain why you should continue in your current capacity. There are already board members suggesting you step down and have me fill in as interim CEO until this whole thing gets sorted out."

He could hardly believe what he was hearing. These were the same folks who, a few days ago, were pushing him to take the CEO role permanently. Now, he felt like they were ready to run him out of town on a rail. And what could he possibly say to make a difference relative to what he was now hearing? Decisively, he offered, "Shane, these are merely baseless allegations. I haven't bribed anyone, certainly not Agent Harper. I'm sure the Feds will come to this same conclusion. We need to wait until this whole investigation bears out what I'm telling you. All of this will simply blow over."

Jack waited for him to speak which didn't take long.

"We can't wait by the phone for the Feds to tell you 'All is well.' We must assure the public, especially our shareholders and the media, that the company is still stable. We will get hammered if we sit idly by and do nothing. I urge you to be at the board meeting tomorrow. To make matters even worse, I'm told we have a potentially aggressive offer to buy Universal. If the press gets hold of this, we could all go down in flames."

He sat back down in his chair, pulled out his notebook, and wrote something down. Then he responded, "How did you know about a potential offer to buy Universal? We received a call only today."

For the first time in the conversation, he sensed he had put Shane back on his heels. He was slow to give a reply, like he was trying to think of an appropriate answer or cover up some hidden truth. Jack didn't say another word. He waited. When he heard nothing, he said, "Are you there?"

"Yes, yes, I'm still here."

Jack noticed Shane's tone was less confrontational. He pressed in. "My question still stands. How did you know about a potential offer to buy Universal? We only came to know about the offer today. And the call only came to one person before I was told. So, what's your answer?"

Weakly, Shane answered, "I got it from a confidential source."

"Who?"

"I promised to keep the source off the record."

"What, confidential from the CEO of Universal Systems? Are you kidding me? I need to know, and I need to know now!"

Now, he got some pushback from Shane. "Look, this isn't the issue. We're talking about some things affecting the stability of the company. I need to go. But let me remind you to be at the board meeting tomorrow afternoon."

"For sure I will be there."

"We need to find a viable solution to this mess."

"Right."

The call ended and Jack pondered the conversation. He realized he had more questions than answers. Since it was well after eight, he decided to text Gloria again and tell her he was leaving the office and heading home.

CHAPTER
TWENTY-SIX

GLORIA WAS SITTING IN THE den reading a book. She had the television on with the sound turned low, but she could still hear it. She looked at her phone to see what time it was. It was well past seven, and she hadn't heard from Jack. By now, he would either be home or would have texted her with his ETA. She thought it was a bit odd and uncharacteristic for him. She put down her phone and was about to pick up her book when she heard in the background a news update, something about Universal Systems. She picked up the TV remote, rewound the news from the beginning.

"We are following the breaking report that one of Universal Systems top executives is being investigated by the FBI and The Justice Department for allegedly bribing an FBI special agent. The name of the special agent is not being released at this time. But what we do know is Jack Alexander is the Universal Systems executive being investigated. Alexander, the current President of one of Universal's divisions, was recently named interim CEO because Lenard Shapiro was recently in a car crash which almost took his life. The details of the investigation have not been released and both the FBI and Universal Systems refuse to comment. We will provide you with more details as this story continues to develop. In other news…"

Gloria sat there, stunned at what she'd just heard. She thought to herself, "*This can't be about Jack. Bribery…this cannot be real. There's got to be a logical explanation for this. He simply wouldn't consider bribing anyone, certainly not an FBI agent. Where is he anyway? Why isn't he home already?*"

Her phone buzzed, letting her know she had a text message. It was from Jack.

> **G, sorry I'm not home yet. I am heading home now. I should be there in 20 minute or less. Love J.**

Gloria was about to send back a text detailing the news report she'd just heard. Before she initiated the text, she thought it would be best to wait until he got home. She said a quick prayer, then picked up her book and tried to continue reading but with no success. She had only one prevailing thought…"*What's going on here?*"

****

Gloria heard the garage door open. She decided to get up and greet her husband. It took him a couple of minutes to get in the house. She walked up to him, hugged him, and gave him a kiss. He returned the hug and she sensed him hold her a bit longer. She moved back slightly and said, "How are you? Long day, huh?"

"Babe, it was one of the most difficult days I've had in a long time."

"Well, I saw a news report about you being investigated by the federal government for bribery charges. What's going on? Why am I just finding out about this whole thing?"

Jack stood still, looked Gloria in the face, took her hand, and said, "Babe, you are correct. I should have told you early about this whole ugly situation. I'm so sorry. In a sense, I was hoping it would all blow over, but it hasn't. In fact, it has intensified. Let's sit down in the den and I'll tell you all the sordid details."

They both sat down, and he explained to Gloria the whole thing, leaving nothing out. When he finished, for a while neither of them said anything. Gloria got up, put her arms around Jack's neck, and hugged him so tightly he was having trouble breathing. Eventually, she released her grip, sat down again next to him, and held his hand.

It was only then he saw the tears welling up in her eyes. She said, "I am so proud of you for trying to help Len and Clarence. You are such a true and loyal friend. This causes me to remember one of the reasons why I married you. Thank you for telling me everything. Frankly, I agree with you. The Feds will conclude what I already know, you are not a man who would bribe anyone. I am so sorry you are being put through all this. So, what's the next step, Babe?"

He thought about his answer and then said, "Honestly, I'm not sure. I will likely know more after my meeting with the board tomorrow afternoon. Tom is handling the response to the Feds. I'll see what he includes, he is more skilled at this than anyone in the company. But the biggest thing you should be assured of, I won't keep you in the dark anymore. Okay?"

"Yeah, thanks for saying that. It makes me feel a bit better. But I won't completely settle down until this episode is over. Look, why don't I make you some food? You must be starving."

"Babe, uh-uh. I'm not hungry and it's too late to eat a meal anyway. Let's go upstairs and get ready for bed. We could maybe read before we go to sleep."

"Are you sure? I'm happy to whip up something, maybe a little snack?"

"Absolutely not, I don't need a thing. Let's go on up."

With that, Jack took her hand, turned off the lights, and they made their way up to their bedroom. After they retired for the night, he lay in bed with so many thoughts roaming through his head. When he looked at the clock and saw it was after one, he forced himself to turn off his brain, and he prayed for sleep and rest.

TWENTY-SEVEN

THE NEXT DAY, ON HIS way to the office, he made a series of phone calls. He had Len, Clarence, Tom, and Matthew on his list. In the conversation with Len, he detailed the Feds' investigation and his upcoming meeting with the board of directors. Len listened and provided him with some valuable insight. They also discussed the potential meeting with OMS who wanted to buy Universal. To this, Len gave Jack his assessment of the situation. He took his advice to heart and promised to circle back with Len once he was further along.

Jack could tell Clarence was calmer. He indicated he was more confident having Harry looking into the allegations against him. He listened to him explain Harry's efforts. Clarence's increased belief was that Harry would help him get to the bottom of the false claims. During the conversation, Jack told him of the information Fred had gotten regarding the brother of Agent Landers. He could tell he was taking copious notes. Yet, Clarence's biggest concern was whether Harry would run out of time before the hearing took place.

****

While he promised to personally investigate why his special agent was being falsely accused, Harry knew he was putting his career in jeopardy. Yet, he felt Clarence was innocent, and he refused to stand by and watch his best agent get railroaded. He sat in his car with his notepad and started writing down elements of the case. He asked himself, *"Who received the anonymous tip regarding the bribery charges? When had it come in? What was said during the call? Who had interviewed Agent Landers? What did she say was the reason she had waited so long to come forward? I will have to walk softly, or I will only make matters worse. Who else can I trust to help me with any aspect of this? If I use my government security access to any files, how can I keep from being discovered? I need to start from the most common denominator. Information is what I need first. Everything else will flow from there."* Harry wrote down some notes alongside each of the questions he had. Then it hit him. *"I know who can help me, Maria Flores. She is the one person I can place complete trust in. But I need to do a few things before I contact her. Yes, I need to embark on this right now!"*

****

"Will there be anything else, sir?"

"No, how much do I owe you?"

"It will be seventy dollars for the two burner phones and seventy dollars for the two basic phone cards. So, without tax, you owe one-forty. Will this be cash or credit card?"

"Cash."

"Fine, sir. It will take me just a few minutes to ring this up for you. Will you be needing anything else?"

"No, this will be all."

"Here's your receipt, sir. And thank you for coming in today."

Harry walked around the corner, in the opposite direction of his car. He wanted to make sure no one was following him. He spent a few minutes in a woman's clothing store. He asked for some suggestions for an anniversary gift, all the while looking out the window to see if someone was watching him. After a protracted period in the store, he walked out and made his way in a circuitous route back to his car. He got in, looked in the rearview mirror, started his car, and left the strip mall. He drove home, parked, and went inside. Since his wife was at work, there was no one at home. He went to the garage, got a box, moved to his home office, and sat down at his desk. He activated the phones, put one in the box, wrote out some instructions, and sealed it up.

After he finished, he made one phone call. When the party answered, he said, "Say nothing except 'yes' or 'no.' Do not ask me any questions. Do you understand?"

"Yes."

"Great. Walk to your car and go to the rendezvous spot where we have met in the past. Look for a box with your alias on it, in the spot you would expect to find something. Is that understood?"

"Yes."

"Great. Please go and do it now."

With those instructions given, Harry hung up and took the box to the spot he mentioned. He knew he had plenty of time to drop the box and leave. After he did, he found a safe, secluded spot and waited. He was there for slightly more than fifteen minutes and then his burner phone rang. He picked up and said, "Hello, Maria. Thanks for calling me."

"Harry, why the cloak and dagger routine?"

"Good to hear from you too."

"Oh, yeah, good to hear your voice. What's going on?"

"I need to ask you something."

"Okay."

"Can I trust you?"

"Harry, what kind of question is that? Of course, you can trust me. Haven't I demonstrated it over the last ten years?"

"Yes, but I still needed to ask you."

"Okay. So, what's up?"

"Clarence Harper."

"Yeah, what about him?"

"What do you know about him or his situation?"

"I only know what's on the rumor mill. He's up on charges associated with sexual harassment and bribery."

"What if I told you he is being framed?"

"I wouldn't be surprised."

"I need your help to get to the bottom of these charges and get his name cleared."

"Hey, back up! You are getting into a place where only bad things happen at the end of it. Are you sure about this?"

"Look, Clarence is an innocent man, and for some reason, he is being railroaded. I need you to help me prove he is being set up. The principal question I need you to answer is whether or not you will help me?"

There was a long pause. Neither of them said anything. Harry realized Maria was weighting the pros and cons of diving into this situation. He knew she would think it was, at best, a landmine. Eventually, he heard her say, "Harry, because it is you, I will help you as best I can."

"Thanks. I wouldn't ask you if I could do this myself."

"Okay, where do we start?"

Harry spent the next thirty minutes devising a plan of action. Maria asked lots of questions and Harry answered each one. At the end of the call, they agreed on how and when they would communicate going forward. When Harry hung up, he was confident he'd made the right decision by having Maria help him. His first task was to get a copy of the charges against Clarence. This was easy. He went into Clarence's file and pulled down both charges. Since Clarence worked for Harry, no one would suspect anything. He was able to download the file to his computer, put the information on a flash drive, and make a copy as well. He had completed the first phase of his plan.

He walked outdoors, found a quiet place, pulled out his burner phone, and dialed Maria. When she answered, he said, "Let's meet at the rendezvous spot we agreed to. I have some things to cover with you. When can you get there?"

"Give me an hour."

"Great, I'll see you then."

When he arrived, the two of them sat down, and he gave her a copy of the file. They were silent as they both spent time reviewing the charges.

Maria was the first one to speak. "My assessment is the bribery charge is completely made up and the sexual harassment might have been coerced. I am surprised the agent who received the anonymous call regarding the bribery charges didn't spend more time trying to track down where the unidentified call came from. It seems the agent took what he received at face value without doing any real assessment of the facts. Regarding the harassment charges, we need someone to get close to Agent Landers and cause her to talk openly and honestly about the issue. We might be surprised at what we find."

CHAPTER
TWENTY-EIGHT

HARRY WAS ASTONISHED BY THE analysis Maria made. It caused him to reflect on her background and all his years of knowing her.

After graduating with degree in Criminal Justice, she got a law degree from John Marshall Law School and went to work for the Chicago Police Department. Not long afterward, she became a detective in the Counter-Intelligence division working specifically with the FBI HUMINT (Human Intelligence area). HUMINT is defined as any information that can be gathered from human sources. To be successful, officers in this area must understand one of the most complex aspects of accumulating assets—human nature. Emotions, intentions, and motivations differ from person to person and change over time. Understanding people with their complexities is crucial to the business of accumulating assets to collect HUMINT. Maria worked with this unit for three years. During her time with HUMINT, she'd worked with Harry. She demonstrated her unique ability to analyze, communicate, and secure vital information from people, namely CIs, confidential informers. Harry was able to crack multiple cases based on information acquired by Maria. Her abilities exceeded those of every agent Harry had ever worked with. After she went back to working for the Chicago Police Department exclusively, Harry continued to reach out to her whenever he had an assignment requiring her skillset. So, it was no surprise when he reached out to her in this case associated with Clarence.

CHAPTER
TWENTY-NINE

H E LOOKED OVER AT MARIA. After she rendered her analytical comments, he said, "Thanks, this is helpful. Now we need to move to the next phase of our inquiry. I need you to determine how to get information from Agent Landers. She will be reticent about giving you, or anyone else, information about the harassment charges against Clarence Harper. But to salvage his reputation, we will need to get her to tell you what actually happened."

"Happy to give it a shot."

"What, if anything, do you need from me?"

"Where will I find her, and what does she look like?"

"No worries, I will send you a complete write-up on her. I'll send it to our secure email connection we've used in the past. Anything else?"

"Oh, one other thing, I will need some FBI identification. I know I run the risk of being 'found out,' but she needs to know I am legitimate."

"Look for a package at the same spot where you found the burner phone."

"Great, I'm all set."

****

Maria got all the requested information from Harry. She sat in her apartment reviewing it. She went over it several times until she knew all she needed to know about Agent Carla Landers.

Harry found out Agent Landers would be in Chicago over the next three or four weeks working on a local case. So she spent the next few days following her. Everywhere she went, Maria was not far behind. She staked out her condo. She observed all her comings and goings.

After ten days of trailing her, they got a big break. Because of the case she was working on, Agent Landers was on call and had to notify her partners where she would be 24/7. She indicated she would be off on the upcoming Wednesday and hanging out with some friends. Harry saw her reports and determined she would be going to a bar. He got the name, location, and the timeframe. He passed the information over to Maria.

On Wednesday evening, she changed her clothes, left home, got in her Toyota Camry, and drove to the spot where Agent Landers was going to hang out with her girlfriends. She walked into Maude's Wine Bar in the West Loop of Chicago.

As soon as she got inside, she saw Carla with three ladies sitting at a table in a remote part of the restaurant. She waited for the hostess to come over and ask if she had a reservation. When Maria indicated she did and another person was going to be joining her, the hostess asked if she had a seating preference. Maria selected a spot where Carla could see her. A few minutes later, her guy friend, Thomas Cordero, arrived. He was a private investigator who had worked with her in the past. Maria had talked to him previously about what she wanted him to do.

Thirty minutes after they were seated, on cue, Maria raised her voice and said, "Where do you get off saying such a mean, cruel thing to me. Get up and get out!"

Her male plant didn't move. He replied, "You need to calm down. I only spoke the truth. I know it and so do you."

Maria got up, reached over, and slapped him in the face. He grabbed her arm and slammed her into the table. Carla was watching all of this and remained seated until Maria got pushed severely onto the table. She jumped up and, using her Bureau training, maneuvered the guy to the floor. A big dishwasher and a burly busboy arrived and escorted the guy out of the restaurant. Carla helped Maria up and sat her in a chair. Maria watched Carla waved to her girlfriends to stay at their table. They looked at each other and then Carla asked, "Are you all right?"

"I think so. I really appreciate you coming over to help."

"No guy should ever toss a woman around like that…but you did slap him pretty hard."

Carla and Maria looked at each other and then they both smiled. Maria said, "Hey, he deserved it."

Maria watched as Carla extended her hand and said, "My name's Carla Landers, what's yours?"

Maria took her hand and replied, "I'm Maria Flores. I'm glad to meet you."

They sat together for about twenty minutes, and eventually her girlfriends got up, walked over to Maria's table, and one of them said, "We decided we're going to head out. We'll talk later in the week. Have a great evening."

They walked out, leaving Carla and Maria. After an hour had passed and they'd had a couple of drinks, Maria could tell that Carla was comfortable talking to her. Eventually, Maria said, "Thanks again for coming to my aid."

"So, what was it that caused such a stir between you two?"

Maria didn't speak right away. She put her head down, and when she looked up again, she had tears in her eyes. She could tell Carla was struck by what she saw.

"Hey, I'm sorry, I didn't mean to pry and make you upset. Forget I asked."

Maria wiped the tears from her eyes and replied, "No, no, it's okay. I'm just hurting right now. Give me a minute, I'm okay with telling you, since you came to help me. Honestly, I haven't told anyone about this except the jerk who left here. He was supposed to be a really good friend"

Maria took another minute to seemingly compose herself. Then she said, "My youngest sister has had a run-in with drugs. She got involved with the wrong people and started doing some things our family never approved of. I am the one closet to her, and I have been trying to help her. Recently, she got into real trouble."

She stopped talking and again put her head down. She heard Carla say, "Maria, you don't have to tell me. I understand."

"I'm okay. I do need to tell someone. It turns out my sister went with two men to steal some drugs, the whole thing didn't go well, there was a fight, one of the men she was with picked up a gun and shot somebody. The guy died and now they want to pin the murder on her because she was there. I got a call, and I took a flight to Dallas to try and help her. Some people told me I could save her if I agreed to implicate an innocent woman in the company where I work. Because I wanted to rescue her, I agreed to do it. Now a good woman is up on charges which could impact her family and cost her some jail time. On one hand, I regret what I did. On the other hand, I was able to help my sister. The guy who I had the fight with told me I was a hypocrite, a fraud, and a liar. I got so upset I slapped him, and you saw the rest."

Maria could see that Carla was shaken by what she heard. She looked at Carla as she sat back in her chair, rubbed her eyes, and then looked around the restaurant with no point of focus. Finally, she responded, "Maria, I am really sorry."

"Well, to make matters worse, now this woman's life is going to be ruined because of what I did. I can't forgive myself. That guy who was here was right. I am a hypocrite."

Maria could tell that Carla was trying to steady herself. She watched closely as Carla put both hands on the table, looked Maria in the eye, and said, "Like you said, you don't know me, but it is interesting how our lives happened to intersect, and how we have some things in common. I shouldn't be telling you this, but I think you need to know you are not such a bad person."

"In common, what do you mean?"

"Well, I had a similar thing happen to me. I have a brother living in the DC area. He, too, got involved in drugs. I had been trying to get him into a recovery program. He tried twice, but both times he failed and went back to a life of drugs. Recently, he gave drugs to an underage girl, and the girl OD'd. He was arrested and was going to be tried for murder. I went there to try and help him. Some people met me and told me if I would help them with a situation, they would be able to get the charges dropped. Without thinking, I agreed to help them. All I had to do was allege that a colleague had sexually assaulted me. The charge was false, but I agreed to do it so my brother could go free. Now I have potentially wrecked a man's life and that of his family."

Maria realized Carla had now told her exactly what she wanted to hear. Now she reached out, touched Carla's hand, looked at her, but didn't say a word. She wanted to hear what Carla would say next. Her next words were, "I shouldn't have told you that story. I did it because I wanted you to know I understand your pain."

Maria waited until she was finished, and then said, "Carla, I now completely understand what you meant by our lives intersecting. Believe me, your story is safe with me. I feel so much better knowing there is someone going through a similar situation. It makes me feel like we are sisters in a way."

She observed the expression on Carla's face, one of amazement. Maria could tell she had never considered the possibility of someone having such a comparable story. Maria needed to seal the relational aspect. So, she calmly said, "If you ever need to talk, here's my cell phone number. Thank you again for coming to my aid."

"Maria, thank you too. I feel like a heavy weight was lifted off my shoulders."

They ended up walking out of the restaurant together. They hugged each other and then went in opposite directions.

CHAPTER
THIRTY

MARIA SAT IN HER CAR, reached into her purse, pulled out her tiny recorder, and pressed the Play button. Instantly, she heard Carla's voice clearly. She advanced the recorder and listened to the key parts telling the reason why she'd accused Clarence Harper. Once she had heard enough, she shut off the recorder, put it back in her purse, and called Harry.

He picked up after a couple of rings. "Hey Maria, what's happening?"

"It worked...I got it all on tape. Our setup created just the right atmosphere. Once she heard my 'tale,' she felt compelled to tell me hers. I believe we have what we need."

"Did she ever asked where you worked or what you did for a living?"

"Nope, we became like best friends after the incident. I gave her the cell phone number I use in these situations. It will show up benign if she ever checks it out. She may call me to get back together for another 'bonding' experience."

"Great, see you on Tuesday. Thanks."

"No worries, I'll see you then."

Harry hung up the phone and thought, *"One down and one to go. The information associated with Agent Landers turned out to be easier than I thought. But I had one of the best people in the business working on it. We still need to confront her with what we know. But I'm still troubled by a couple of things: who was it that approached Agent Landers and why did they want to place blame on Clarence? I believe if we crack the code on these bribery charges, I'll have my answers. This one won't be so easy. I sense we'll need a big break of some kind."*

****

Tom had completed the response back to the Feds. Based on the outside counsel he received, Tom felt confident the Feds' issues would likely evaporate. He was more concerned about the potential intended offer to buy the company. On the phone, he told Jack again of the multiple calls he had received from OMS regarding a meeting to discuss their offer. Tom said, "I don't know how we can ignore them. We don't want this to turn into a hostile takeover, especially with the bad press regarding the allegations. So, what would you like me to do?"

"Let's hold off until my meeting with the board this afternoon. I'll have a better answer then."

"Okay, I'm fine with that, but let me know as soon as possible."

"No worries."

Jack hung up and called Matthew's number; he picked up immediately.

"Thanks for calling me. If you hadn't called, I was going to reach out to you."

Jack sensed the tension in Matthew's voice. Normally, he was calm and relaxed. But he could tell Matthew was breathing quickly and there was a sense of nervousness. He told him, "Matthew, slow down, take a minute, and then tell me what's going on."

Matthew didn't speak right away. Eventually, he said, "I am getting calls from this guy, Javier Moreno from OMS Corporation. He's asking me financial questions with an assumption we will negotiate the sale of Universal Systems. I didn't answer any of his questions and referred him to your office. He then called me back twice with additional questions. This guy won't take *no* for an answer. What's your advice?"

He considered the question and then answered, "First off, Matthew, you did the right thing by directing this guy to my office. If he calls back again simply tell him, 'This is abuse and I won't stand for it.' You can also tell him his harassment will likely sour any possible chance of a deal between our two companies. Understood?"

He waited for Matthews to reply. He said, "Yes, I understand."

"Great! Be sure to let me know immediately if he calls you again."

"I will for sure."

CHAPTER THIRTY-ONE

JACK'S MORNING WAS FILLED WITH conference calls and internal meetings. He did have to field some calls from worried account teams, clients, and larger investors about the bribery allegations. He did his best to waylay their concerns, letting them know there was no truth to the Feds' investigation. His intercom went off, he answered, "Yes, Beth, what is it?"

"I have Michele Thompson on line one."

Michele had been the Vice President of Client Services until Brian Franks left the company for a Senior VP role with another firm. She got promoted to Vice President of Sales and Marketing. In her new capacity, she grew sales by 21% in her first year at the helm. Jack picked up the line and said, "Hey, Michele, it must be really important."

When Michele took the new role, she and Jack developed this joke: "Hey, you'll never hear from me unless it's really important."

"Thanks for taking my call. And, yes, it is important. I have been receiving calls from salespeople asking me about the rumors regarding the Feds' bribery charges. I have been handling all of them until I got a call from the Brazilian Country manager. He says three of his largest clients are threatening to end their business relationship with us over this. I tried to assure them the rumors were baseless, but they aren't confident the clients won't walk."

Jack listened to everything Michele had to say. He knew the three clients and the revenue they represented. He said, "How widespread is this in the company?"

"I'm not sure."

"How quickly can you put this information together for my review? I need to know the negative impact this rumor is having."

He waited while Michele thought about her answer. She finally said, "I can have the report put together for you by tomorrow morning. When would you like to meet?"

"Check with Beth and find an open slot on my calendar. I need to address this immediately."

"Great! I'm on it."

"Oh, Michele, thanks for calling me. I appreciate it."

"Sure thing."

Jack hung up, leaned back in his chair, put one hand on his head as he closed his eyes. He thought, *"This is big! The last thing we need is for companies to start bailing on us because of this issue with the Feds. I need to see the total impact before I decide what to do."*

He kept his eye on the time because he wanted to get to the conference room before the board members started to arrive for the special meeting. He had gone over every possible detail. He was leaving nothing to chance. Yet, he realized the decision to have Shane take over the CEO role temporarily would be left to the board. He had already spoken to a select number of board members, ones he thought would agree with his desire to remain CEO during the Feds' inquiry. He decided to stand as the board members started filing into the room. He remembered how Len would greet each person and have some special remarks. He tried to follow Len's relational model. Every board member was cordial to him, some more than others. Shane was a bit cold, but Jack didn't let it deter him. After twenty minutes of casual conversation, Shane called the meeting to order.

"Okay, let's everyone take a seat so we can get started. As you know, I called this special meeting because of the recent accusations brought against Jack. Bribery is a serious charge. I've asked him to come and share his thoughts on these charges and where they came from. The question before us is whether we leave Jack in place as our interim CEO with these accusations hanging over him, and negatively impact Universal, our stock price, and our investors, or replace him temporarily until this business with the Feds comes to an end."

Jack looked at each board member. He tried to read their facial expressions and body language to determine how Shane's comments sat with them. For the most part, they appeared neutral.

"It is no surprise I have made the recommendation for me to take over the CEO role until he is in the clear."

Jack now realized Shane had saved this part until the end of his remarks.

Shane slowly let his last words hang in the room for effect. Then he concluded with, "So, let's have Jack contribute his thoughts before we take a vote to try and save this company."

His eyes were on Shane as he turned toward him, smiled, and said, "Jack, what would you like to add?"

Jack stood up, walked to the head of the room, looked at each of the seated board members, and steadied himself. He recognized this was a critical moment. Whatever he said now would greatly impact the board's decision. He began slowly, not wanting to rush. "Shane is right. You should replace me. And he, as the current board chairman, is the perfect choice to be my replacement."

He wasn't surprised by how stunned every board member was by his words. He stood still and looked in the face of each person, one by one. Several seconds went by as what he'd said sunk in. Then he continued, "But, you see, if we do what Shane is suggesting, we'd have real turmoil. It would be the second CEO change in less than a month. Our stockholders, the media, our clients, and especially our employees would feel a real sense of instability. So, the very thing he wants to avoid, we would be diving headfirst right into. Ask yourself, 'What's happening here?' I'll tell you. There are some unknown forces attempting to create chaos in this company. If we give in to this pressure, we will be creating unnecessary havoc for all concerned. Shane suggests we make a change only until the charges, which are utterly baseless, are dropped. Here's what you don't know. The Feds received an anonymous tip, which can't be substantiated. Our CFO, Matthew Warren, has already determined the audit trail is totally bogus. I have always appreciated the collective wisdom of our board. Now is the time for us to see the wisdom in not operating in fear. Let's not make any rash or hasty decisions. We would do well to remain strong in the face of adversity. When all of this is over, when it's proven to be in error, everyone will see us as strong in the face of adversity. Thank you for listening."

Rather than sitting down again, he stood tall, looked at each person, and added one more comment. "I leave you to make your collective decision. I trust you will be strong and courageous."

With his final remark, he walked slowly out of the meeting. As he closed the conference room door, he made his way back down the hallway to his office.

CHAPTER
THIRTY-TWO

THE REST OF THE DAY was filled with more attempts by Jack to convince major clients Universal was not in trouble and the Feds' investigation was baseless. He knew he would hear from Shane by the end of the day. He was content to adhere to whichever way the board decided. He was making his to-do list when his cell phone buzzed. It was Tom. He immediately picked it up.

"Tom, what's going on?"

"I just got off the phone with Javier Moreno from OMS. He is pushing for a meeting with us to seriously discuss the acquisition of Universal. He says if we refuse to meet, they will go to our shareholders to make their case."

He listened and waited until Tom finished. He asked, "I sense there is something you aren't telling me. What is it?"

"You may not have looked recently, but our stock took a real tumble today. Apparently, the news about the alleged bribery charge has created a sell-off. We are in a very precarious position right now. By the way, have you heard anything from the board? Somehow, we have got to make some decisions."

Jack concluded Tom was right. He needed to make some choices, and now was the time. He said to Tom, "Fine, check with Beth and set up a meeting with the people from OMS. Let's face it head-on. And, no, I haven't heard from the board yet. I was told I would hear something by the end of the day."

Jack waited to see if Tom had a reaction. When he didn't, he continued, "I am confident the stock price will rebound once the Feds' investigation is over. So, until then, we must proceed based on the current situation."

"I will reach out to OMS, set up a meeting, and send all their information to your private email address. Be on the lookout for it."

Jack was about to respond when he realized he had another call coming in. "Tom, I've got to hang up. Keep me posted."

He hung up and switched over to the incoming call. "This is Jack Alexander."

"Hey Jack, this is Shane. I told you I would call you with the board's decision."

He sensed an abruptness in his voice, but he remained cordial. "I appreciate your efforts as we sort things out during this trying period."

He then stayed silent to hear what Shane had to say. "We spent a while contemplating our decision. It turns out your comments to the board were very compelling. I stressed to them the importance of protecting the company, and everyone involved. However, the board voted to keep you in the position of CEO. They believe it is for the best and making a change at the top would prove detrimental."

It was only then Jack realized he had been holding his breath. He let out a sigh of relief. Then he said, "Thanks for calling me and giving me the board's decision. Were there any other things decided?"

"Yes, in fact, there was another thing. There have been rumors about an offer to buy the company. If the rumors are true, and if there is an upcoming meeting, the board wants me to be a part of it."

"As you know, we regularly get offers to buy the company. If there is a bona fide meeting, I will make sure you are included."

With those words exchanged, the call ended. Jack sent a text to Gloria letting her know he was wrapping up things and heading home. He was still reflecting on the call as he took just a few minutes to tidy up and head for the elevators. As he rode down to the parking garage level, he kept remembering the earlier conversation with Shane. *"How did he know about the offer to buy the company? Who did he get the information from since only Tom knew about it?"*

As he got out and started the short walk to his car, an ominous feeling came over him. He felt like he was being followed. He turned around twice and each time there was no one there. He looked in the direction of the parking lot cameras. Realizing they were there, he felt a bit more comfortable. A few feet from his car, he hit his key fob. The double beep let him know the doors were open.

Just as he reached for the door handle, a bag was roughly put over his head. The bag seemed to be made from some coarse material and it extended down to his neck. He called out, "Hey, if it's money you want, my wallet is in my left coat pocket."

He opened his right hand and offered, "You can have my car, here are my keys."

He heard nothing from his assailant. He was shoved up against his car door and his hands were pulled behind his back. Then he heard, "I'm only going to say this once. You will make every effort to sell Universal. You will be as complicit as possible, it's your choice. But if you don't, you and your family will be negatively impacted in the worst way. Oh, one more thing, if you breathe a word of this to the cops, you will regret it. Now, put your hands on the roof of the car. Put your head down, and don't move until I say so."

Jack was terrified. He followed the instructions and waited for what he would be told to do next. He couldn't tell how much time had passed, but he tried not to move. Eventually, he called out, "Listen, I've followed everything you've asked. Please let me go."

He heard no reply. He continued to wait. Unsure, he took his right hand off the car and placed it by his side. When nothing happened, he reached up and took the bag off his head. He looked around and determined he was alone. The assailant was gone.

He picked up his keys from the garage floor, opened his door, got in, and then he started shaking and sweating. His mind rushed to all the possibilities of something worse happening to him. He looked around a final time, put the key in the ignition, and started his car. The air conditioner clicked on and started to cool him from his harrowing experience. He said a prayer thanking God for his safety. Putting the car in drive, he drove out of the garage and headed home. He was still shaken up, but he felt relieved to be driving. His thoughts were all over the place. *"Do I call the police and potentially put G at risk? Do I remain quiet and let whoever it was sense they were able to intimidate me? It is clear Universal is at stake. Lord, help me to make the right choice."*

At that moment, his cell phone rang. It was Clarence. He answered the call. "Oh, my goodness, thank you for calling me. I really need to talk to you right now."

"What's up?"

"Honestly, things are happening so fast, my head is spinning. I don't know if I'm coming or going. However, in the strictest of confidences, I'm going to tell you what just happened to me."

"Okay…"

Jack detailed what took place in the parking garage. After he finished, he asked, "What do I do?"

"For sure, calling the police is not a viable option. Yet you need protection for you and Gloria. I want to be crystal clear. I could easily agree to become your bodyguard and protect you and your wife, given the fact I'm on administrative leave. But because of the bribery charges, I would be doing us both a disservice by trying to protect you at this point. Nonetheless, I have a friend who owns a personal security company. I'm going to give him a call. I realize your children are out of state. I will get him to provide protection for them as well. So, expect a call from Arnold James. He will refer to my name. Trust me, he is exceptional at what he does."

"Thanks, I was stumped regarding what to do. I hope and pray this option works."

"Believe me, it will. Now get on home, give your wife a kiss, and stop worrying."

"Thanks again."

"We'll talk soon."

CHAPTER
THIRTY-THREE

"WHAT TIME IS THE MEETING set for?"

"Ten a.m., Mr. Santos."

"Who's going to be there?"

"Tom Wallace, their general counsel, Matthew Warren, their CFO, and Jack Alexander."

"Wait, isn't that board chairman going to be there as well?"

"Oh yes, Shane McCarthy will also be there. I know we were hoping he would convince their board to sideline Alexander until the Feds' investigation was over. But it didn't work out that way. Apparently, this Alexander guy made an impressive argument for why he should continue as CEO. We knew it would be a fifty-fifty shot. Shane tried but came up short. We at least have him at our meeting today."

"He's merely window dressing for us anyway. What time do we need to leave here?"

"Your car will be downstairs at nine-thirty. We'll get there in plenty of time. But we will walk into the meeting fashionably late."

"Fine, come back for me when it's time to leave."

As Javier walked back to his office, he mentally went over all the items he needed to address at the upcoming meeting. Armando was relying on him to communicate the essential elements of their offer. All the facts and figures had been well-rehearsed in his mind. Yet, he had to keep them arranged in the order Armando specifically required them to be. This was, by far, the largest and most important deal he had ever been a part of. As he made his way to his office, he reflected on how he had arrived at OMS.

He'd grown up in Mexico, in the state of Zacatecas. Each state in Mexico had multiple municipalities; his was called Pinos, which was also the name of the town where he was born. His town of 5,100 people was moderately poor. Most families lived on less than five dollars a day. Modern conveniences like electricity, piped-in water, indoor plumbing, and televisions were common in his town. However, less than half the families in Pinos had cars, and even less had a landline or a mobile phone. Technology hadn't fully taken hold in the town as fewer than 10% had access to a personal computer, and even less could utilize the Internet.

He was the youngest of three boys. Both his mother and father could read and write, but never finished grade school. His father, Juan Moreno, started working in the town's only factory as a teenager. He met Anna at a church dance, and they got married nine months later. Javier's brothers followed a similar path as their father. He got them jobs at the local factory so they could help the family. Anna wanted a different life for her young son, Javier. He graduated from grammar school. When his father announced it was time to work in the factory, his mother objected. There were several nights when arguing could be heard between his father and mother. In the end, his mother wrote and called one of her aunts who had immigrated to the US and lived in Chicago. She pleaded with her to sponsor her son, let him live with her, and attend high school. The day his visa was approved, there were mixed feelings in the Moreno household; his mother was ecstatic, his father was reserved and quiet, his siblings said little, not knowing what to say. A few weeks later, Javier's dad drove him to the bus station for his long ride to the United States. His brothers said their goodbyes, his mother spent the entire time reminding him of all the things he needed to do. "Be respectful to your Aunt Daniella, keep your room clean, finish all your chores, study hard, write to me every week, and make us proud."

All Javier said was, "Yes, Mama, yes Mama, and yes Mama."

His father never said a word. He carried his only suitcase into the bus terminal, gave him an envelope, looked him sternly in his eyes, clapped him on his back, turned toward the exit door, and walked away. The bus ride from Zacatecas to the border was 48 hours; two days and nights. There would be another two days before he finally arrived in Chicago. It gave Javier lots of time to consider the significance of this journey.

Seven and a half years later, he had graduated from high school and college with a degree in business. As he promised, he wrote to his mother every week. Part of the money he earned he sent back to Mexico to help his family. After his graduation, his business class mentor introduced him to Armando. The two of them hit it off and he got hired into the company's management training program. Javier worked his *butt* off, received a series of promotions, went to graduate school at night, and eventually became the head of Mergers and Acquisitions. Armando relied on him, and Javier continuously rose to each occasion. As he sat down at his desk, he repeated his standard mantra: Don't just strive to be the Best, *be* the Best. At five feet nine, one hundred and seventy pounds, and jet-black hair parted down the middle, he didn't have the most intimidating image, but his amazing presentation style more than made up for it. Today, he would remind Armando again why he'd hired him and promoted him to this position.

However, Javier had another pressing issue. He had a gambling addiction. He had never really gambled before but some friends from college held weekend parties in their dormitory. While he lived off campus, he was invited and attended them. It was during those festivities he was introduced to gambling. Initially, it started off as a social-bonding activity. Later, he started taking trips to Las Vegas during spring break. After college, he developed a strong predilection for card playing. He alternated between 3 card poker, Mississippi Stud poker, and Texas Hold 'em. Little by little, the stakes grew as well as his addiction. He found a local card game near his West Loop condo where they played for big money. He would regularly take out a line of credit from the House if the cards didn't go his way on a particular night. Generally, he would pay off his debit within a week. The last time he played, he lost a lot of money. He owed the House $40,000. He felt confident he would be able to pay it. Armando had committed to give him a substantial bonus based on their last acquisition and the work he had done associated with preparing for the Universal Systems acquisition. The first problem was, he started getting calls, first asking when he would pay up; then they turned into threats, and finally he was told about the interest charges they were adding to the debt. The second problem was if Armando found out about his gambling debts, he would be fired immediately. So, he needed the acquisition of Universal to happen posthaste.

CHAPTER
THIRTY-FOUR

JACK SAT AT HIS DESK looking out his window at Lake Michigan. He could see boats moving effortlessly in the water; some were speedboats, others were sailboats, and one large vessel called *the Odyssey*. He reflected on pleasant times aboard the ship; team outings, noisy luncheons, and an anniversary evening cruise with Gloria. He looked out farther toward the horizon and saw storm clouds brewing. He couldn't tell how long it would be before they reached the shoreline. He also couldn't determine the intensity, but he knew it was coming. At that moment, he realized he had a sense of foreboding about this upcoming meeting with OMS, especially given the assailant's words in the parking garage: *"I'm only going to say this once. You will make every effort to sell Universal. You will be as complicit as possible, it's your choice. But if you don't, you and your family will be negatively impacted, in the worst way."* He didn't know how intense it would be, but he knew it would be a challenge. So, in his mind, he needed to prepare for the worse. At that moment, his intercom buzzed. He picked up and Beth said, "I have Michele Thompson here."

"Send her in."

"Yes, but I need to remind you Tom and Matthew will be here in forty-five minutes."

"Okay, when they arrive, let me know."

He hung up and almost immediately his door opened, and Michele walked in. Michele was quite tall for a woman. She stood six feet and had a very athletic build. Jack remembered her backstory. She just missed qualifying for the US Olympic team in the Heptathlon. As a black woman, she had every intention of following in the footsteps of Jackie Joyner-Kersee. But right now, she had a worried look on her face.

"Michele, come on in and have a seat."

He waved her over to the side table. She sat down, turned on her laptop, pulled out a report from her briefcase, and steadied herself. Then she said, "Jack, I had my people provide me with their list of clients who have expressed concern associated with the bribery rumors. Then I ranked them based on revenue contribution. Finally, they were segmented based on market. So, what you have in front of you are the top twenty-five clients based on those three factors; expressed concern, revenue contribution, and market. They represent the greatest risk for us as a company."

Jack perused the list without responding. He immediately noticed the top fifteen clients were in the United States, the UK, and South America, especially Brazil. He said, "First, thank you for quickly putting this together. Second, it is very comprehensive. It shows our greatest exposure, which is exactly what I needed. Now, what is your recommendation as to how we deal with this?"

Michele was hesitant as she considered his question. She looked down at the report, rubbed her hands together, and then looked up at Jack. She replied, "I think you need to go and see them, express your sentiments, and reassure them the rumors are baseless and unfounded. Your presence is a critical ingredient. It is not enough for the Country Manager to tell them. They need to hear it from 'the horse's mouth.' Also, the sooner you do it the better. Some of these accounts have already had other firms whispering in their ears. We need to cut this off now!"

Jack found himself rubbing his hands, almost in the same way Michele had. He realized the sensitivity associated with this issue. He also needed to consider the implications of him being away while the Fed's investigation, the board's consideration, and the issues facing Clarence were going on. This wasn't a simple decision. Yet, the company's revenue and profit were at stake. He picked up the report, stared at Michele, and said, "You're right! I want you to set these meetings up personally. Let's try and fit this into a week of travel, not longer. If I need to take 'redeye flights,' I'll do it. Work with Beth to move around other meetings to accommodate this. I'm trusting you to make this happen, understood?"

Michele didn't miss a beat. She replied, "Absolutely. I'll get right on it."

She put her papers together, stood up, shook his hand, and started walking towards the door. Before she turned the knob, Jack said, "Michele...I know you won't let me down. I have great faith in you."

She smiled, turned, and was about to walk out when Jack added, "Oh, one more thing. Once I get back from the trip, I want you to get with Matthew and create a report detailing how each division will end the year. Being totally open with you, I committed to Len that my divisional plan for JPC was to double revenue and make it 60% more profitable than last year. I'll be particularly interested in these data points."

"No worries…I'll take care of it."

As soon as she walked out, his intercom went off. He picked up.

"Tom and Matthew have arrived."

"Send them in."

The door opened and, with purposeful strides, the two of them walked in.

"Guys, come on in and take a seat. Let's get right to it. How much time do we have before our meeting with the OMS folks? And do you know who is coming to the meeting?"

Tom was first to speak. "Javier Moreno, their head of Mergers and Acquisitions, and Armando Santos, their CEO. As you know from the documents you received, Armando is also the son of the company's founder. They will be here in less than an hour. What other questions do you have for us?"

"You tell me…what else do I need to know?"

"You need to be cognizant of the fact our stock price has taken another extreme hit based on the news about the Feds' inquiry. OMS will try to take advantage of this fact. Our stock opened this morning at three-twenty-four a share, which is down twenty-six percent since the story was released by the press."

"Got it. What else?"

"They are likely to go to our stockholders if we don't play ball with them."

"Wait, wait, so selling the company…is this what you are suggesting?"

"We need to understand the condition we find ourselves and have a strategy to counteract their or any other attempt."

Jack looked at Matthew and said, "You've been quiet this entire time. What's on your mind?"

"I'm new here. I take my lead from you. However, I do believe the stock will rebound once this FBI business is over."

They spent the balance of their time before the meeting discussing their strategy. When they finished, they packed up and headed for the conference room.

Beth met both Armando and Javier in the reception area and led them to the conference room. Jack, Tom, and Matthew stood up, walked over, and introduced themselves. Everyone sat down after all the introductions were made.

Shane walked in a couple of minutes later and took a seat "Sorry I'm a little late. I got hung up in traffic. What did I miss?"

Jack said, "No problem, we just started. This is Armando Santos, CEO of OMS, and this is Javier Moreno, Head of Mergers and Acquisitions." Pointing to Shane, "This is our board chairman, Shane McCarthy."

He continued, "Armando, you wanted to meet with us to discuss your interest in acquiring Universal. We'll let you state your intentions."

Jack watched Armando's every movement and every facial expression. Len had taught him how to look for body language, which expressed desire and intent. He could tell Armando wanted to project a cool, calm, and relaxed exterior. It was clear from his mannerisms he was used to being in control.

He leaned back in his chair and folded his hands just below his mouth. He looked the four Universal folks in the eye before he spoke his first words. Then he said, "I'm here to buy Universal Systems."

Jack could tell he wanted to set the tone of the meeting, so everyone knew it was his show. He let his first sentence hang in the air.

He continued to look at the four of them before moving on. "We are prepared to take over the company one way or another. We are happy to spend time negotiating with you. But, make no mistake, in the end, we intend to take over Universal Systems."

Jack sat there with his eyes on Armando, and he said to himself, *"There's his phrase again...to take over. It is clear there is no beating around the bush with this guy."*

Armando continued, "Every other company we have determined to acquire, we have obtained. Such will be the case with Universal Systems. Javier will go over the details of the offer. My intent is to complete this transaction as quickly as possible."

He watched him turn to his cohort and add, "Javier."

There was no break in the action. Javier stood up and walked to the other side of the conference table. He passed out copies of a document they were seeing for the first time. He started with, "Here are details of our offer to purchase Universal. I will walk you through each page and entertain all questions you have."

Jack opened the document as Javier sat down and started going through it. The presentation of the information, the questions and answers took almost two hours. All during the meeting, Jack watched

Armando. He was looking for any telltale sign of what might be going on in his head. Nothing stood out. There was nothing he could latch on to.

Then Javier asked, "Well, what are your thoughts? As Mr. Santos said upfront, he wants to complete this matter as quickly as possible."

Jack realized it was his time to speak. He looked at Armando and said, "First of all, we appreciate you coming in and presenting your offer. To be honest, we have had other offers in the past to acquire our firm. We haven't seriously entertained any of them. We have no plans to sell the company. Nonetheless, we will huddle and determine our response to your offer. Again, thank you for coming in."

Once again, he glanced at Armando's facial and body language for a 'tell.' He saw none. He waited for either of them to respond. When neither spoke, he started to push back his chair from the table. Then he heard Shane say, "Mr. Santos, I was impressed by your presentation and your offer. I can promise the board will give it our full and complete consideration."

Jack was appalled. Why did he feel it was his place to say anything? His comments were so unnecessary. Again, Armando said nothing.

Jack stood, walked over to the other side of the table, and shook hands with both of them. He repeated, "Thank you again for coming and extending to us your offer. As promised, we will get back with you. I must run to another meeting I'm already late for. But Tom will walk you out. Have a great rest of the day."

For the first time, he noticed a slight 'tell' in Armando's eyes. He could see him squinting when Jack said he had to go to another meeting. Clearly, it indicated Armando felt slighted and was angered by being handed off, in his mind, to an underling. Jack simply smiled, opened the conference room door, and disappeared down the hall. He said to himself, "Gotcha."

THIRTY-FIVE

N THE CAR, ON THE way back to their office, Armando turned to Javier and said, "Get to our guy and have him put some more pressure on this Jack Alexander. I'm not sure he gets it yet. I didn't like his cavalier attitude. He needs to know we mean business. I want this deal done yesterday."

"I'll make it happen."

****

Jack settled into reviewing the documents Beth indicated were urgent. It had been over two hours since his meeting with the OMS folks. His intercom went off and Beth announced that an Arnold James was in the lobby to see him. She stressed the fact he had no scheduled appointment. Jack told her to show him in. He remembered Clarence telling him Arnold James would be coming to see him. Beth opened his office door and ushered him in. He looked the part of a bodyguard. He was six foot three, about two hundred and twenty pounds. It was clear even with his clothes on, he was fit. As he walked into Jack's office, he had a confident swagger, not cocky, but self-assured. He was dressed in a well-tailored, expensive, gray herringbone suit. He wore a white shirt, no tie, but with fancy cuff links. His eyes were a hazel color with specks of gold, green, and brown in the center. As he walked closer, nothing missed his purview.

Jack was the first to speak. "Mr. James, how can I help you?"

"Mr. Alexander, Clarence Harper asked me to do him a favor by providing you with personal security from now until the unforeseeable future when it is determined you and your family are safe. I should warn you my services aren't free, but I will forgo the elaborate screening process because you are a friend of Clarence's. By the way, my friends call me Arnie."

"Point well taken. I appreciate you agreeing to take me on as a client. Oh, and likewise, my friends call me Jack."

The two of them looked at each other and simply started smiling.

They sat down at his side table and for the next hour discussed the current situation, the assault in the company's parking garage, the Feds' investigation, the car accident with the CEO, the board meeting to keep his job, and the current company takeover attempt.

Arnie said, "Thanks for the update. It's clear you have a ton of issues. I now realize Clarence was right, you need a personal bodyguard."

"Arnie, tell me about yourself, your company, and anything else I should know."

"I grew up in a rough part of town in the District of Columbia. I had a choice between street life and the military. I joined the army right out of high school. College wasn't an option since my folks couldn't afford to send me. I'm the oldest of five children, and my folks had to make some tough choices. Without going into elaborate details, I did two tours in Afghanistan, seven years in Special Forces, left the army, went to college on the G.I. bill, got a bachelor's degree, and seven years ago I started my own security and protection agency."

Jack was impressed with his background. He asked, "Special Forces… were you like Rambo?"

His naivete made Arnie smile. He replied, "Rambo is a movie character. Special Forces training constitutes fifty-three weeks of intense discipline like unconventional warfare, small unit tactics, language, and cultural training, and so much more."

Jack persisted, "So, what did you actually do in Special Forces?

"I basically did what I was instructed to do. But my primary responsibilities were in Covert Ops, Hostage Rescue, and Counter-Terrorism."

"Well, clearly, you are the expert in this area. How do we proceed?"

Arnie didn't hesitate. "First, wherever you go, I go. You are never without me. If I say we don't go into a room, an elevator, a car, or any place else, we don't go. I always have the final say. If you are in a meeting and I don't think it's safe, you leave on my command, no questions asked. These items are non-negotiable. Are we clear?"

He could tell from Arnie's words, the tense and grave expression on his face, he was serious. Jack responded, "I'm clear and I concur. Whatever you say goes."

He noticed a slight head nod from Arnie. Then he added, "My services are twenty-four-seven, and it will cost you five thousand dollars a day, with a six-month minimum. You will provide my firm with a two-hundred-thousand dollar retainer up front."

Jack reflected on the contractual requirements briefly and then said, "I'm fine with the financial agreement. When can you start?"

"I will have the contract sent over to you today. If you put in place all the requirements, I can start tomorrow."

"What about my family. What would be the arrangement?"

"It will be detailed in the documents you receive later today."

"Perfect."

Jack hit the intercom and said, "Beth, when my meeting is over, please see to it Mr. James has everything he needs immediately. Also, be sure to include him in the trip plans Michele is arranging for me."

He stood and Arnie followed suit. They shook hands, Arnie turned, walked to the door, opened it, and softly closed it as he exited.

Jack thought to himself, *"He's the most unusual person I have ever met. But somehow, I feel safe already."*

CHAPTER
THIRTY-SIX

UPON ARRIVING HOME, JACK explained the security and protection plans he'd put in place, as well as his upcoming trip. Gloria asked a few questions. Nevertheless, he could tell from her relaxed facial expression, soft eyes, and a slight smile on her face, she was comfortable with the arrangements. He neglected to tell Gloria about being assaulted in the parking garage. With all the other things, he didn't want to raise her level of anxiety and be worried every time he walked out the door, bodyguard or not.

*****

The next day before Jack's morning run, the black sedan that had followed him a few days earlier was parked in a very inconspicuous spot waiting for him. As Jack opened his front door, he came face-to-face with Arnie James.

"What are you doing here at my home at the crack of dawn?"

"A better question is, where do you think you're going?"

"On my morning run."

"Not today and not for the foreseeable future. This *run* of yours is a perfect place for you to find yourself in trouble."

Jack was about to object when he remembered their agreement. Instead, he said, "Would you like to come in?"

"Sure."

"I guess if you got up and came to my home this early in the morning, you probably haven't eaten breakfast."

"Nope, I haven't."

So, he gave Arnie refrigerator privileges, went upstairs, let Gloria know Arnie was in the house, showered, dressed, and went back to the kitchen. He arrived just before Gloria came down. He found Arnie sitting at the kitchen table with a complete breakfast of coffee, cereal, eggs, bacon, and French toast.

"I didn't realize when I gave you refrigerator privileges, you would take it to these extremes."

"Well, I figured we needed to eat. So, I made breakfast. Sit down and dig in."

When Gloria appeared, Jack turned and said, "Gloria, I want you to meet Arnold James. You should know, Babe, his friends call him Arnie."

He then looked at Arnie and said, "This is my wife, Gloria."

Arnie stopped eating, stood up, and walked over to Gloria, and extended his hand. He said, "Gloria, it is an honor and a privilege to meet you. It is clear you are Jack's better half."

Gloria shook his hand and replied, "Arnie, good to meet you too. I have a few things to ask you and a few things to say."

Arnie looked straight at her. "I would be happy to spend some time talking to you. Please, come sit down and have some breakfast. I hope you enjoy it."

Gloria walked over, grabbed a plate, put food on it, pour herself some coffee, and sat down across the table from Jack and Arnie. She wanted to make sure she could see them both while she talked to Arnie. "Jack told me you will be his personal bodyguard and your firm will also protect our family as well. I am thankful for your intervention. Yet I need to know how you will ensure safety for all of us."

Arnie put down his fork and placed his hands comfortably in his lap. He had a slight smile on his face, and he nodded as a way of acknowledging her comments and concerns.

She continued, "I want to know about you and your company's experience in the protection business. My husband and my family are critically important to me. What assurances do we have that all of our family members will be sheltered from harm?"

Arnie sat perfectly still, in a relaxed, yet attentive manner, and waited for her to finish. When it was clear she had completed what she wanted to say, he took his time in responding. "Gloria, thank you for your comments and your expressed concerned. I absolutely agree with you regarding having assurances associated with your family's protection and safety. Let me say it is my objective to keep you and your loved ones safe. My firm has been providing these services for individuals, families, and companies for years. Having spent several years in the military, and specifically Special Forces, I have gotten the nation's best training in this area. Every person in my firm has been expertly trained in protection. These are the reasons Clarence Harper recommended me to your husband. We will take every precaution to ensure your safety. What other questions do you have?"

Gloria listened to everything Arnie said. Nonetheless, when he mentioned the Clarence Harper's name, her manner and posture changed. She had the deepest appreciation for Clarence. Not only was he a valued friend, but he had rescued Jack and saved his life when he was kidnapped. So, if he recommended the man sitting in front of her, she felt she could trust. She said, "Fine, thank you for your explanation. I feel a bit better about what we are getting into. But remember, I need you to make sure this man"—pointing at Jack—"is protected at all times."

Arnie listened and then quickly responded, "Gloria, let me assure you, along with you and your family, he is priority one."

Gloria had not touched her food. After Arnie's last comment, she reached over and picked up her fork. She started eating and didn't say anything for a few minutes. She was amazed at how good the food and coffee tasted. She commented, "This food is great, and the coffee rivals my own. Where did you learn to cook like this?"

"Army food was the worst. So I set up a little cooking station in our barracks. While it was against regulations, our CO didn't seem to mind. In fact, the Commanding Officer would come by for his share of food as well. I have been cooking ever since."

With a smile on her face, she said, "Well, thank you for saving me the trouble of having to make breakfast today."

Jack realized the break in the conversation and the time. He interjected, "Babe, I need to get to the office. So, Arnie and I need to leave. If you are ready to go, we should head out. You said your car was parked around back."

Arnie was first to speak. "Yes, I'm ready. I'll just put these dishes in the sink and run some water over them. I'm sure you folks have a dishwasher."

Gloria spoke up. "Arnie, of course we have a dishwasher. Please leave the dishes on the table. You guys can get on with your day. 'J,' please call me later."

Jack got up, picked up his jacket and briefcase, walked over to Gloria, bent down, kissed her, and said, "Sure, Babe, I will call you this afternoon. Have a great day. I love you."

"I love you too."

In the car, Arnie discussed with Jack his earlier observations. "When I was driving here, I noticed a black sedan parked with two guys sitting in it. My radar went off and I determined they were watching your house, probably waiting for you to go for your *run*. You might have encountered some difficulty on the running trail today."

It took a moment to fully comprehend what Arnie said. Then he replied, "Could you make out who they were? Did you get a license plate number? We should probably check them out."

"There was no point in making it obvious I was watching them. I'm sure they saw me walking up to your door. However, I did get a partial license plate. We'll see what we get from it. This way, they won't see us leave."

Jack thought to himself, "*This guy is good.*" Arnie concentrated on driving and left Jack to his thoughts. About halfway to the office, Arnie spoke. "Tell me more about the incident that happened in the parking garage."

After Jack detailed the encounter with the assailant, Arnie said, "I went to the security office to look at the footage from the cameras in the garage. It turns out the cameras had been tampered with where your car was located. I couldn't see what happened. All I can conclude is the guy was a professional. So, we need to be extra careful."

They arrived at Jack's office well in advance of his first meeting. Shane came by to strongly suggest Jack consider the OMS offer. "With the stock price currently in the toilet, the OMS offer looks good. Plus, you get to stay on as Co-CEO throughout the transition."

He listened intently to Shane's comments. When he was done, Jack asked, "Why are you passionate about selling the company to these folks? What's up?"

Jack watched him look away as if trying to determine what he would say next.

"I simply want the best situation for Universal. We don't want to wait until we only have a no-win option."

"Got it. Thanks for coming by."

"Okay, but you need to strongly consider my suggestions. By the way, what's happening with the Feds' inquiry?"

"Nothing to report. Believe me, I will keep you posted. I've got an appointment and I don't want to be late."

He could tell there was some reluctance on Shane's part to leave. But he disappeared almost as quickly as he had arrived. Jack hit the intercom and said, "Beth, please ask Arnie to step into my office."

"Sure thing."

Virtually no time passed before he appeared.

"Arnie, I wanted you to know I have to visit the former CEO of Universal, Len Shapiro. There are some things I need to discuss with him, but I don't want to risk it over the phone. This is one meeting you don't have to attend with me. I can handle it."

He saw the stern look from Arnie. He said, "When I established my ground rules, I told you wherever you go, I go, no exceptions, unless you want to end our contract."

"No, I don't want to end it. I just thought…"

The look on Arnie's face said it all.

"Fine, let's get going."

The ride to Len's house was uneventful. Neither Jack nor Arnie said anything aside from the basic directions and the address. He called Len and confirmed their arrival time. He also indicated someone would be with him but didn't say who.

When he arrived and he had introduced Len to Arnie, they had a long and in-depth conversation. By the end of it, Jack felt it had been beneficial. It had started to get dark outside by the time they left. Jack suggested they take the tollway since it would be faster. It turned out to be a bad decision since the I-Pass lanes were closed for repair. The Cash Only lanes were at a virtual standstill. As they waited for the lines to dissipate, Arnie noticed the same black sedan four or five cars back. He immediately assessed the situation, opened his glove compartment, took out a gun, and handed it to Jack.

"Listen carefully. Those two guys from this morning at your house have been following us in the same black sedan. I'm not sure how they tracked us. If they somehow followed us to your office this morning, they could have put a tracking device somewhere on my car without me realizing it. Nevertheless, I need you to follow my instructions explicitly. Understood?"

"Yes, but what am I supposed to do?"

"You see the little tollway house on the other side of the expressway? When I tell you to go, I want you to run as fast as you can to the backside of the building. When you get there, get as low to the ground as you can and find a safe spot. If you hear noises, fire off a couple of shots to stop whomever it is in their tracks. When I get to where you are, you will know it is me because I'll say 'Jackie, it's Arnold!' Have you got it all?

"Yes, I hear you loud and clear. So, what now?"

"Not sure yet, we'll have to keep an eye out. It's their call."

Jack could see, in the side view mirror, the black sedan, now only four cars back. Suddenly, the guy on the passenger side got out of the car and started heading toward them. He was walking at first, then he started a slow jog.

Arnie announced, "Okay, get out of the car now and do exactly as I told you. Go now!"

With the gun in the waist of his pants, Jack hopped out of the car and started running for the tollway house Arnie had pointed to. He had little trouble crossing over the lanes because the cars had either stopped or slowed down considerably. He looked quickly to his right and could see the guy from the black sedan chasing him. It didn't take much for him to outdistance the guy. He was immediately thankful for the early morning running he did.

The tollway house was rectangular. When he got to the building, he ran around the back. There were big fifty-gallon drums stacked on top of each other in multiple spots. He picked a spot farthest away and ducked down behind them, remembering Arnie's instructions. From his vantage point, because of the angle of the lights on the building, he had a clear view of anyone coming around the corner. He was full of anxiety; his hands were shaking, and he almost dropped the gun on the ground. He couldn't imagine who was chasing him and what they wanted. He saw the shadow of someone creeping along the side of the building. Then he heard, "Hey, Jack, it's me. You can come out now. It's safe, they've gone."

Realizing it was a trap, he did exactly what Arnie told him. He pointed the gun in the direction of the image he saw; and fired two shots. Jack could see the man retreat slightly, as if he were reconsidering his options. Then the image disappeared. He kept his eyes peeled and the gun in his hand. He had no idea how long he waited.

He saw another image, raised his gun, and was about to shoot. Then he heard, "Jackie, it's Arnold."

He hesitated for a few seconds. Then he stood up. As he did, he could see clearly Arnie standing a few feet away from him. On shaky legs, he walked toward him.

Arnie covered the rest of the distance between them and took the gun from Jack's hand. "Are you okay?"

"I'm not sure, but I must be all right if I'm standing here and not lying down with a bullet in me. What happened?"

"Those guys were definitely the ones who were sitting near your house this morning. The guy who remained in the car pulled over to the shoulder, got out, and headed for me. After I sent a few warning shots in his direction, he got back in his car, cut across three or four lanes of traffic, picked up his buddy who chased you, and they took off. This time I got the full license plate number. I'll check it out later tonight. In the meantime, let's get you home. I can tell you're a little shaken up."

CHAPTER
THIRTY-SEVEN

"**WHAT! HAVE YOU HIRED BUMBLING** idiots? They were supposed to put the fear of God into the guy. Instead, he nearly shoots one of your imbeciles. Catherine, I told you I would not tolerate any slip-ups. And you assured me there would be none."

She offered no defense. She simply sat and listened to Armando's tirade. He was correct. The two guys sent to shake up Jack had fumbled the job. But no one had foreseen him hiring a bodyguard. They thought he was merely a new driver, a chauffeur. She'd done some checking and come to realize he was ex-Special Forces. So, now they were dealing with a professional and Jack was on *red alert*. Her goons had missed their window of opportunity to terrorize him. Who knew he would have a gun?

Eventually, he stopped his harangue and said, "Catherine, what's your plan at this point? I figured by this time we would be close to a deal. I recognize now we are no closer to buying Universal than before I arrived at their offices."

She hesitated before responding. She had to appease him and assure him her plan was airtight. He would not tolerate a second setback. "Mr. Santos, I deeply apologize for the unfortunate impediment to your plan. You have my word it will not happen again."

"What's next?"

"First, we will get to our friends in the Press to do another series regarding the on-going Federal investigation of Jack Alexander and *other unknown accomplices.* Second, we'll have their Board Chairman reach out to significant stockholders and convince them they should embrace the sale. Third, our people are already talking to some of Universal's largest clients, via an established backchannel, about halting any additional services until the Feds' inquiry is sorted out. Fourth, via the same backchannel, we have some key managers and employees ready to resign due to the ongoing investigation. Our fifth approach is for these employees to demand his resignation. Oh, we also have a little surprise arriving at Jack's home. This will finally convince him to sell."

Catherine stopped, took a deep breath, and waited for him to respond.

After a prolonged silence, he replied, "I see. So, when will all of this be put into action?"

She had come to understand a basic element of Armando's nature. If he liked something, he would start asking questions. Catherine had the feeling she was back on solid ground again. She responded by saying, "Our timetables are set. With your approval, we can start the first phase today, and the other pieces will subsequently be put in place. Rest assured; the purchase deal will rapidly be on its way to completion."

"For your sake, there had better not be any more false starts or you will find yourself in a bad way. Do I make myself clear?"

"Absolutely! "

"The sooner the better. This is priority number one, regardless of what we need to do to get it."

The call was over. Catherine disconnected from her secure line and put her phone back in her purse. Her thoughts were on the details of what she'd described to Armando and his subsequent demands. She knew all the events and the required timetables. Now she had to make them happen or accept the consequences and Armando's wrath. After some reflection, she picked up her phone, turned it back on, and surveyed her text messages. There was only one she was interested in. It read,

> **We are all here in the lobby and ready to come up.**

She replied,

> **Great, take the elevator to my floor and convene in my room. We will begin immediately.**

CHAPTER
THIRTY-EIGHT

JACK SAT NEXT TO ARNIE on their American Airlines flight to Rio de Janeiro. He reviewed his itinerary while Arnie slept. Michele and Beth had done an amazing job structuring the meetings with the top fifteen companies representing the greatest loss risk to Universal. He and Michele had agreed he should meet with each of the chief executives at those companies and reassure them there was nothing to the bribery rumors. As he looked over the information, it was clear he would be all over the globe over the next seven or eight days. He'd be worn out when it was over, but it was worth it. The first set of meetings was in Rio. RTO was the primary company he was visiting. However, there were two other firms in the city. While they were not on the list of fifteen, they were on the list of twenty-five. So, it was determined he would meet with the other two firms since he would already be there.

Michele made a special note to Jack letting him know he should not be surprised by the high-end fashions worn by the senior executives he would meet in Brazil, including the employees at Universal Systems.

He opened the first folder, which was RTO. As one of the largest logistics operators in Brazil, they had a huge network of ships, railroads, trucks, and ports used to transport their clients' products. Their CEO, Riccardo Gabriel Alvarado, had been in the company for twenty years, the last five as the CEO. His rise in the organization had been steady. He was smart and had a way of building strong relationships with people he led and others he interfaced with. People genuinely liked him. He could be tough, but he was very fair. It was clear from the press clipping: he was a strong CEO. The company had realized some of its best years under his leadership.

Riccardo came from very humble beginnings. Both of his parents were poor coffee farmers in the state of Minas Gerais, which means mines of the general woods. They didn't earn very much money. The average coffee worker had no rights whatsoever. Virtually every laborer knew they were being exploited but felt they had no choice in a country of rising poverty and scarce jobs.

When Riccardo was born, they determined to save as much money as they could to ensure he got the best education possible. During his grammar school education, he showed tremendous promise. He had the second highest grade point average during his high school education. He was accepted at Universidade de São Paulo, the best university in Brazil. Four years later, he graduated at the top of his class. Based on his educational progress and the recommendations from educators and high-ranking officials, he was offered a full scholarship to acquire his master's at Access Masters, also in São Paulo.

Before he started working on his advanced degree, he got a job and for a year he earned money to help his parents. When he received his master's, he was recruited by several companies around the world. He decided on RTO because he wanted to stay in Brazil, be close to his parents, and RTO promised him the opportunity to compete for the top spot in the company. Based on the significant financial performance of RTO under Riccardo Alvarado, he was written up in major magazines around the world. He was repeatedly asked to be the keynote speaker at conferences throughout Central and South America. One of his key business focal points was to build relationships with partners who could add value to his company. Based on a valued endorsement, he retained Bain to be RTO's management consulting firm. However, there were some significant misalignments and he decided to replace them. Based on a tremendous set of presentations and strong client recommendations, he, personally, made the decision to hire Universal Systems' consulting division JPC to replace them. RTO had become Universal's largest client in South America. The relationship had gone well until the bribery rumors started. Jack knew he needed to make a positive impact on Riccardo to retain their trust and their business.

Arnie started to wake up. He looked over at Jack and determined he probably hadn't slept. "Jack, this is going to be a long week. There is so much riding on every one of these upcoming meetings. So, it is critical for you to get the proper rest. You can't burn the candle at both ends, my friend."

"No doubt. But I need to know all the pertinent details well in advance. I won't have a second chance to make a first impression."

"Yeah, and I don't want their first impression to be you falling asleep in their conference room."

Jack was about to respond when he heard, "Sir, is there anything I can get you?"

Jack looked up and saw the smiling face of their flight attendant. "No, I think I'm fine. But I do have a question. What time do we arrive in Rio de Janeiro?"

"We will land and be at the gate in an hour and a half, about seventy-thirty a.m."

"Thanks"

CHAPTER
THIRTY-NINE

ARNIE GOT UP AND HEADED off to the restroom. Jack closed the file he was reviewing and opened another one. He looked at the picture of Eduardo Fernandes, the Country Manager of Brazil for Universal. The file indicated Eduardo would be meeting Jack and Arnie at the airport, taking them to the three meetings, and driving them back so they could make their flight at the end of the day.

Eduardo had been with Universal Systems of South America for seven years. He had come from a competitor and was hired as a first-level manager. He had two priorities during his first three months with the firm: figure out the personnel he needed to get rid of and meet with every existing client to determine what they needed from Universal.

He had one-on-one meetings with each person on his team. He asked them to present their accomplishments over the last twelve months and what their strengths and weaknesses were. Eduardo was shocked by what he heard and saw. Half of his team had no real accomplishments and the strengths they outlined were mediocre at best. In addition, only four people had acquired a new client over the last year. More than half of the clients he met had not been thrilled with the services they had received over the past year. As a result, they were not enthusiastic about the relationship with the Universal team.

Eduardo got rid of the poor performers, hired talented replacements, and built his new team around the four people who had been holding up everyone else. He also had secondary meetings with every client, apologized for Universal's poor services, asked them what they needed, and put together individual client plans to deliver on his promises. In addition, he worked with his team to secure new clients. His new team had the best performance in South America over the next year. So, management decided to expand his responsibilities. Someone mentioned to management Eduardo's name meant "Guardian of Prosperity." He succeeded in every role he was assigned. When the previous Country Manager quit and went to another firm, Eduardo was asked to interview for the role. The interview team loved him, and he was hired. For the past two years, his operation had exceeded their quota year-over-year by 40%. Client satisfaction was at the highest in the history of the operation.

Michele and Beth had told Jack he should text Eduardo as soon as his plane landed. Following their instructions, Jack sent a text.

> **Eduardo, this is Jack Alexander. We have landed here in Rio de Janeiro.**

He waited for a couple of minutes before receiving a text reply.

> **Thank you for your message. Now you should proceed to Customs. Once you have finished and have gotten your luggage, walk out of the airport through gate three. I will be waiting for you there.**

It took about twenty minutes to get through Customs, pick up their luggage, and walk out of Gate Three. Eduardo Fernandes walked up to them. He was five foot nine and about one hundred and seventy-five pounds. He had dark brown hair and brown eyes. His round face had bushy eyebrows. He wore a gray Giorgio Armani virgin wool, two-piece suit, a sharkskin weave. It had a notched lapel, two-button front with a double-vented back. His attire included a classic white shirt, a gray striped tie, black Caporicci Italian shoes, and silver cufflinks.

"Welcome to Rio de Janeiro, Señor Alexander. It is good to meet you and your...uh, friend."

"Eduardo, thank you for coming to get us. Two things: you can call me Jack, and this is my associate, Arnold James."

Eduardo turned to Arnie and said, "Welcome to Rio de Janeiro, Señor James."

The two of them shook hands and Arnie said, "Thank you, and my friends call me Arnie."

They walked to the car, which was a silver, late model, four door Audi. After they were leaving the airport, Jack asked, "Our first meeting is set for nine a.m. How long will it take to get to Avenida Presidente Vargas where RTO is located?"

"It will take us about twenty minutes. Since it's not yet eight o'clock, we have plenty of time."

"Great. I'd like to sit down and talk to you before our meeting with the client. Will there be a place nearby?"

"Yes. I know just the spot."

FORTY

ONCE THEY WERE SEATED IN a small restaurant within walking distance of RTO, Jack said, "Since I have never met Riccardo Alvarado and I don't speak Portuguese, I will need you to be my translator. However, I will need you to tell me everything he says and communicate his exact emotional subtext. In addition, I will need you to communicate to him the exact words I say and my expressions. What I am requesting is critical to this meeting. Can I trust you to do this?"

Eduardo leaned back in his chair, started rubbing his hands together, looked out at the street, and after a few seconds had passed, he looked Jack in the eyes and said, "Yes, I believe I can do what you have asked."

****

As they were escorted into the RTO conference room, Jack saw two people. He had been told there was the possibility of Ava Delgado, the

Senior Vice-President of Digital Transformation, would be joining the meeting. Jack was given her background, just in case.

Ava had come to RTO just five years ago. She had been recruited to the company by her father, Alesandro, who had worked for the firm for twenty-five years, the last three on Riccardo's management team. He had explained her value proposition to the CEO, convinced Ava to interview, and allowed them to determine if she would be the right fit. Six months after she started with RTO, he retired.

She was highly regarded throughout the industry. She was the oldest of her siblings. Her parents expected her to set the example for her younger sister and brother. From grammar school through college and later, graduate school, she always got the best grades. When she secured her MBA, she had multiple offers across South America. She decided to accept the offer from CEG based on their significant experience in Foreign Trade Assistance and consultancy. The company offered technical substructure to large, small, and mid-size domestic companies, as well as international firms. CEG offered her a huge package, an important title, and an exit strategy she felt comfortable with. She was content in her role until her father started telling her about the advantages of working for RTO. The company matched the stock options she left at CEG. She negotiated hard but, in the end, her father was the deciding factor.

Ava was an attractive woman. She also was a real "clothes horse." From the look of her outfit, she was highly invested in fashion, and it was clear she didn't get dressed in the dark. She had jet-black hair, green eyes, and a cleft in her chin. She was five feet five but the three-inch heels she wore made her seem taller. She wore an Alexander McQueen Bi-Color shirred bow-embellished wool-blend blazer with matching pants. The white blouse, the Roberto Coin 18k gold diamond solitaire stud earrings, the Lana 14k bond-link choker necklace, and the Alexander McQueen black/gold punk spike stud pumps added to her overall ensemble.

The three of them walked up to Riccardo and Ava. Jack was the first one to speak. In perfect Portuguese, he said, "Bom dia, É um prazer conhecer vocês dois. Obrigado por concordar em se encontrar comigo. Você é um cliente valioso da Universal Systems e achei importante viajar até aqui para conhecê-lo Meu pessoal me diz que você está preocupado com os rumores que ouviu. Estou aqui para que você saiba que não tem nada com que se preocupar. Aliás, eu não falo português. Eduardo Fernandes será meu tradutor. Então, vamos nos sentar e ficarei feliz em responder a quaisquer perguntas que você tenha. Eu prometo que não vou embora até que você esteja completamente satisfeito." Properly translated in English, Jack said, "Good morning, it's a pleasure to meet you both. Thank you for agreeing to meet with me. You are a valuable customer of Universal Systems, and I thought it was important to travel here to meet you. My people tell me that you are concerned about the rumors you heard. I'm here to let you know that you have nothing to worry about. In fact, I don't speak Portuguese. Eduardo Fernandes will be my translator. So, let's sit down and I am happy to answer any questions you have. I promise I will not leave until you are completely satisfied."

Both Riccardo and Ava were shocked. They looked as if they had seen a ghost. Their eyes were wide open, their pupils dilated. Their jaws were slack, and their mouths were like a gaping hole. Neither of them could believe what they had just heard. When Jack realized he was traveling to Rio and meeting with the key executives of each of these three clients, he felt he needed to speak to them, at least in the beginning, in their own language. He had rehearsed his speech until he could say it on demand. He didn't ask anyone's help, except Rosetta Stone. The rest of the meeting went exceptionally well.

FORTY-ONE

AFTER LEAVING RTO, THE THREE of them found a coffee shop, sat down, and debriefed the meeting.

Eduardo was the first to speak, "Jack, where did you learn to speak Portuguese? What you did back there was amazing. I had no idea you were going to open with your impressive speech."

Arnie chimed in, "Yeah, my friend, I have no clue what you said, but from the look on their faces, you hit a home run."

"I just determined what I wanted to say and recited it until I knew it cold."

Eduardo said, "Well, I would suggest you begin each of our next two meeting in the same way."

Jack did repeat the opening speech with the executives at the next two meeting. The results were the same, the clients were satisfied with what Jack had to say, appreciated Jack flying in to meet them in person, and they committed to remaining a Universal System's client.

****

As Jack and Arnie sat on the plane, they heard, "Please make sure your seat belts are securely fastened and your carryon luggage is in the overhead compartment or under the seat in front of you. Please make sure you turn off your electronic devices at this time. We ask you now to sit back and relax for the next eleven hours to London's Heathrow Airport."

Jack decided it was time to follow Arnie's recommendations. He kicked off his shoes, covered himself with two blankets, and shut his eyes.

****

Jack and Arnie crisscrossed the globe over the next seven days. In total, they visited fifteen clients. Much like what he had done in Brazil, Jack had rehearsed an opening speech he delivered at the start of each meeting. The customers were impressed by his ability to convey the speech in their native language. Only one customer expressed some hesitation and said they would be watchful over the next few weeks. If the rumors went away and nothing came of them, they would remain a loyal client. So, the trip was a major success. Their last client visit was stateside, in Los Angeles.

Jack kept in communication with his office, and Beth did a great job of keeping in touch with him on the important issues as they arose. He stayed in contact with both Tom and Matthew regarding the feedback from the Feds. It was all quiet. The Feds hadn't been able to find the "smoking gun" they were looking for, but they weren't willing to say Jack and Universal were in the clear.

In addition, he had stayed in daily contact with Gloria. He kept her up to date on his progress and she told him how things were going along at home.

As the plane landed at O'Hare International Airport, Jack was bone tired. While he did sleep on the planes, it was nothing like sleeping in his own bed. Plus, the time zones wreaked havoc on his body clock. He realized he had more to do to quell the rumors, but he had made significant headway. He turned and looked at Arnie. He appreciated having him along for the trip. His presence made him feel both protected and comfortable. There was no concern in his mind regarding his safety. Arnie was like a big brother. There were things he did naturally, things Jack would never think to do. He said, "Arnie, I know the protection you have been providing me is your job. Nonetheless, I want to thank you for performing your role in a superior fashion. During this entire trip, I never felt I was in harm's way."

"If that's true, then I did my job."

"Yeah, I know, but you didn't just go through the motions. I felt you really cared. It's what money can't buy."

Arnie didn't immediately reply. He turned and looked out the window of the plane as if he were trying to determine when they would land. Then he turned back to Jack and said, "I do care about you and your safety. Honestly, there are some jobs where I'm basically on autopilot. I care about the assignment, just not that much. I sense something about you. I believe it is your character. I watch the way you regard people and what you say to them. My sense is you are the 'real deal.' So, I've been trying to keep you safe so you can have the opportunity to complete the things you have on your plate.

And, by the way, I've learned some things in these various meeting we've attended."

Arnie's last comment brought a smile to their faces.

CHAPTER
FORTY-TWO

THE LIMOUSINE WAS THERE TO pick up Jack and Arnie right on schedule. Since it was 9:30 a.m. when they got through Customs, Arnie had time to contact Beth regarding logistics.

She picked up on the first ring and said, "Arnie, how are you? I assume you are both at O'Hare?"

"Correct. We only have a few minutes before we get outside the airport. I need you to answer a few questions, and please be specific."

"Okay, fire away. What do you need to know?"

"What is the name of the limousine service you contracted to pick us up, and what is the name of the driver? I also need to know exactly what he or she looks like."

Beth had the information on hand. "The name of the limo service is Chicago Executive Limousine Services. We have used them multiple times in the past. The name of the driver is Riccardo Torres, but he answers only to Ricky. He is below average height, about five feet seven, he has a birthmark on the left side of his face. It looks like a boot, almost an exact replica of the Italian Boot. We confirmed he would be the one picking you guys up from the airport. Do you need anything else?"

"Nope, that's all. Hopefully, we will see you in less than an hour. Thanks."

Arnie ended the call and turned to Jack. "You need to wait inside the terminal until I give you the sign to come out. If everything is fine, I will give you a thumbs-up signal with my left hand. Remember…a thumbs-up sign with my left hand. If you see anything else, I want you to move away from the door, move quickly to the policeman over by that Starbucks down the hall. Tell him who you are and ask for his protection until I arrive. Are we clear?"

"Yes, I'm clear, but what is causing you to be so alarmed?"

"I don't know for sure, but no one knows we are coming back today except the limousine service. If I had thought through it fully, I would have had one of my guys pick us up. Since the tollway episode, we can never be too careful."

Just then, Jack received a text.

> **Mr. Alexander, we are here to pick you up and drive you into the city. Please look for a black limousine, license number AT 69030. Let me know which door you will be exiting.**

Arnie looked at the text message and instructed Jack to text back.

> **Riccardo, we will be exiting through door number three. Please stand outside the car so I know which limo to come out to. Let me know you got this message.**

They waited for a reply.

Mr. Alexander, I will be waiting for you at door number three. Look forward to seeing you.

They both looked at the text reply and spoke at the same time.

"It's a trap!"

They took the escalator back to the second floor and started walking briskly from Terminal 1, the United Airlines terminal, to Terminal 2, the Delta Airlines terminal. It took them about fifteen minutes. While they walked, Arnie called a number. When he got an answer, he said, "Hey, we've got some trouble here at O'Hare. How quickly can you get here?"

He waited for the answer. He said, "Great, we'll be in Terminal Two, Delta Airlines. Call me when you are within five minutes. Regardless of what security says, pick us up on the upper level. I'll tell you which door we will come out of when you call me back. I need you to be here right now, so step on it."

Once they got to Terminal 2, they found a safe spot where they could sit and see every person at a distance. Realizing they couldn't go back through security; they were in the best place possible.

Ten minutes passed and Arnie's cell phone buzzed, and he picked up immediately. "Yeah…okay. We will walk out of door number two from Terminal Two. Remember, come to the upper level. Uh huh, right, see you then."

Arnie turned to Jack. "Let's move to the door. Now, if I say, 'get down,' I want you to lay flat on the floor, no questions asked. Got it?"

"I hear you loud and clear."

CHAPTER
FORTY-THREE

AS THEY RODE IN THE backseat of the four-door BMW, Jack relaxed for the first time since they'd gone through Customs. He listened to Arnie give instructions to his guys, one who was driving and the other one who sat in the front passenger seat. Once he was finished, he collapsed in the back seat and said nothing for a few minutes. They both listened to the sounds of the traffic on the expressway as they headed downtown.

Eventually, Arnie looked at Jack and said, "How did you know it was a trap?"

"In the text message back to the driver, you suggested I use his full first name, Riccardo, which he never responds to. When he sent back his reply and made no reference to his name, I realized it was a setup. My only question now is, what happened to Ricky?"

"No idea, but the text 'test' worked. These guys were obviously after you. Somebody is trying to send you a message. They probably figured our guard would be down after a long series of flights. You have now been threatened once, chased, and now another thwarted attempt. Someone is obviously trying to get your attention. It all adds up to OMS and their interest in buying Universal."

"Yeah, I'm beginning to agree. But why go through all this?"

"It's my opinion they are trying to get you scared and softened up so you will agree to whatever their terms are. Where else are you exposed right now?"

Jack thought intently about the question. He turned and looked out the window. Noticing the other cars on the expressway, he reflected on the issues he'd been faced with over the last several weeks.

Suddenly, it hit him. He turned back toward Arnie and said, "The one area of exposure is the Universal employees. As I think about it, our employees are very loyal. Yet, these rumors about the Feds' bribery charges probably have some employees wondering if Universal is still a great place to work. Both our stock and our image have suffered of late. I need to address this in the same way I did with our clients. And I need to do it now!"

****

It was a lot to pull together, but Jack had his leadership team put together a series of virtual Town Hall meeting with employees around the globe. He had Edmond Pearson, Vice President of HR, head up the effort. The meetings were staged based on different parts of the company and based on time zones. The intent was for all employees to hear Jack be open and transparent about the rumors. He decided he would explain his recent visits to clients all around the world and his vote of confidence from the board of directors. The most important agenda item was to answer questions in an open, honest fashion.

By the time the last Town Hall meeting was over, Jack was exhausted. Nonetheless, based on the feedback he received both from the management team and during the meetings, it had been worth it. He couldn't stop the media blitz, but he could, and did, communicate his integrity.

CHAPTER
FORTY-FOUR

THREE WEEKS HAD PASSED SINCE the meeting with her team. It had gone well, obvious by the events that had taken place. Catherine was satisfied with everything so far. She had regularly provided updates to Armando, and he was pleased with her progress. Since her plans were making headway, she decided to go for a walk, get some fresh air, and clear her head. The suite where she had been staying, thanks to Armando, was just a few blocks from Lake Michigan. As she headed toward the water, a slight smile crossed her face. Catherine felt confident she had everything under control. For the first time in years, she felt she was about to see the demise of Jack Alexander. She had come close before, but now she could almost see him in his orange jumpsuit being led away to federal prison. Catherine pictured her special unmarked account under her assumed name with $10 million dollars in it. While she still had to report to her parole officer, she was only a few months away from not having to do that any longer. Her biggest desire was to work her way back into the good graces of her daughter, Rachel. She was in a near-euphoric state. Right then, she didn't have a care in the world. As she stepped off the curb to cross the street, she never noticed the light was turning red, and she didn't see the white SUV barreling down on her at fifty miles an hour. Her last conscious thought was what a bright, sunny, carefree day it was.

****

Beep, beep, beep…these were the short, high-pitched sounds of the monitors Catherine was attached to for patient-tracking, respiratory, cardiac support, pain management, emergency resuscitation devices, and a whole series of life-support equipment. She was in bad shape when she arrived at Northwestern hospital. The extent of her medical condition hadn't fully been determined. However, she had multiple life-threatening issues and her heart had failed three times in the last twenty-four hours. Now she was barely conscious.

One of the ICU nurses was checking on her and noticed she was awake. She said, "Oh, Ms. Frazier, how are you feeling?"

It took Catherine some time before she could answer. She mustered up as much strength as she was able to and said, "I hurt. What happened to me? Why am I here?"

"You were hit by a car. You were in such bad condition; the paramedics were not sure you would make it."

"When will I be released?"

"Ms. Frazier, you've been here for four days. You'll have to ask the doctor how long you will have to stay. But, honestly, based on the severely of your injuries, you'll be here for a lot longer."

"I have to get out of here. I've got some critical things to do. I need you to find the doctor right now!"

Even in her weakened condition, Catherine was forceful. She was groggy and having a hard time staying conscious. However, in her current condition, she thought about Armando, his demands, and the status of all the things she had been orchestrating. Four days was four days too long. Catherine fell off to sleep. When she woke up several hours later, the doctor was just walking in. He first looked at her chart and then he slowly approached her bedside. With a smile on his face, he asked, "Ms. Frazier, I'm Dr Thomas, how are you feeling? You had been unconscious for a long time. There were times when we thought we had lost you. We're all glad you're back."

"Doctor, I need to know when I can leave here."

She watched the doctor's smile change to a worried frown. He pursed his lips slightly before he spoke. "Ms. Frazier, you experienced some traumatic injuries. It took an entire medical team to get you stabilized. As a result, I have no idea when you will be able to leave here. We are still completing tests to determine the full extent of your injuries."

"The full extent of my injuries…what have you determined thus far?"

Catherine could tell the doctor was uncomfortable with her question. He looked away, then down at her chart, and then finally peered into her eyes. He replied, "You sustained incredibly significant injuries from the car accident. As near as the paramedics could assess, you were hit by an SUV, you were hurled in the air, and your head struck the pavement severely. We took fluid from your brain because it started to swell. There is still more we must do. We didn't think you would regain consciousness. Your thorax, abdomen, spine, pelvis, and your upper and lower extremities were greatly impacted. From all the trauma, your heart stopped multiple times. The car ran over both your legs and knees. There is more. But I think I'll stop to give you time to process what I've told you so far."

Catherine was extremely upset. It was hard for her to comprehend the full extent of her injuries. Still very woozy, she tried to compose herself. Then she asked, "So, Doc, you're on a roll, what else?"

She watched him hesitate to speak. He again looked away and then down like he was studying her chart again. He then said, "Somehow, you have a punctured lung. We're not sure how extensive the problem is. Nonetheless, based on the series of tests we've done thus far, you'll need some additional surgery to stabilize your condition. So, again, we just aren't sure how long you will be hospitalized."

He took a deep breath, not sure how she would respond.

She looked at him and asked, "Doc, you said the SUV ran over my legs and knees. Will I be able to walk again?"

"We're not sure right now. So, my advice to you is to rest up and we will tell you more as we learn more."

Based on the condition of her legs, Catherine couldn't roll over on her side, away from both the doctor and the nurse. So, she turned her head, shut her eyes, and tried to block out the world. She was thrown into an immediate depressed state. She kept thinking about all the things the doctor had told her. She thought, *"How could this be happening to me? The last thing I remember was being on top of the world. And now I'm lying in a hospital bed with these physical challenges. Plus, no one even knows I'm here. I need to get in touch with Armando. He needs to know where I am and how I got here."*

She turned her head and hit the nurse's call button. When she came in, Catherine said, "Since no one knows I'm here, I need to get in touch with someone. I'm sure they are worried about me."

"Okay, I know where your belongings are. I'll get your phone and bring it in to you."

When the nurse left, Catherine thought, *"I'll call Armando and then I'll get in touch with my daughter Rachel."*

CHAPTER
FORTY-FIVE

"**C**ATHERINE, WHERE HAVE YOU BEEN? I've called you multiple times. I guess this venture of mine wasn't important to you."

"Not true. The same day I last talked to you; I was hit by a car and have been in Northwestern Hospital ever since. Today is the first day I have been awake. I don't have any health insurance and I am basically alone."

There was silence on the line. Catherine needed him to respond. Finally, he said, "You are on your own. I have no idea what you expect from me, but I can't and won't help you. I told you if anything went wrong, I would cut you off."

She was shocked by what she heard. She knew he was heartless, but she was positive he would come through for her given her dire situation. "What? You can't abandon me like this. After all I've done, I would think you would come to my aid."

"After you literally disappeared, I had to scramble to keep my affairs on track. You let me down. So, no, I can't help you."

"But I got hit by a car, I was unconscious, and I have multiple life-threatening injuries. You've got to help me. I'm begging you to show some compassion."

She waited for him to reply. She thought he was weighing her passionate plea. When she heard nothing, she said, "Armando, Armando…are you there?"

It was then she realized he had hung up. She was despondent and then she was livid. She thought, *"He hung up. He is a cold-blooded mongrel. Why did I even bother calling him? At this point, my only option is to contact my daughter. I pray she will be more sympathetic."* Hesitantly, she punched in Rachel's number. The phone rang several times and then went to voicemail. Catherine left a message and then hung up. She started feeling lightheaded. She only heard, 'beep, beep, beep.' It was the last thing she remembered.

****

"Northwestern Hospital, how can I help you?"

"Yes, please get me up to the floor where Catherine Frazier is hospitalized."

"Okay, please hold on."

"Hello, this is the nurse's station in ICU, how can I help you?"

"Yes, I am checking on the condition of Catherine Frazier. Can you please tell me how she is getting along?"

"I'm so sorry but we aren't able to provide any information unless you are a family member."

"I understand completely. I am Catherine's brother, Tony. I'm out of the country and a close friend told me she had been hospitalized. I'm checking on her condition to determine if I should change my plans and come back to Chicago."

"Mr. Frazier, I understand. I hate to be the bearer of bad tidings, but she is in very poor condition. The doctors don't give her much chance of surviving the next few days. So, if you want to see her before she passes, you should get here as soon as possible."

"Oh, thank you so much. I will make every arrangement possible. I appreciate your help."

"Sir, you are welcome. Let us know if we can serve you in any way."

"I appreciate your offer. But you have already helped immensely. Have a good day."

"You too, goodbye."

Armando hung up the phone and smiled to himself. He thought, *"Well, I don't have to concern myself with her anymore. Given her condition, she'll be gone soon enough."*

****

Catherine woke up to the sound of beeping and hissing monitors. She slowly looked around. It took her a few minutes for her eyes to adjust to the light in the room. She saw someone in the room, but she couldn't determine who it was. However, she decided it was her nurse. She said, "Nurse, I need something to drink and another blanket."

She heard someone say, "I will hit your call button. Your nurse will come in and I'll ask her to get what you need."

"Who are you?"

"We have never met."

"Who are you?"

"Your doctor asked me to come in and see you."

Catherine started to get agitated. She asked again, "Why can't you tell me who you are?"

"Oh, sorry. I am Pastor Thomas, one of the chaplains here at the hospital. But my friends call me Sheila"

Catherine thought about what she heard for a moment and then asked, "Okay, Pastor...Thomas, what was the doctor hoping you would do here since I didn't ask for you?"

"I'm told your name is Catherine Frazier. Can I call you Catherine?"

There was a pregnant pause. Finally, Catherine whispered, "Yes, you can."

"Well, Catherine, I make regular rounds throughout the hospital talking to patients who have experienced significant trauma. I was told about some of what you have gone through. Could we spend a few minutes just talking?"

Catherine simply looked at her, did not answer, and thought about the question. Finally, she said, "What do you want to talk about?" She noticed a smile start to form on Sheila's face.

Then she heard her say, "Well, let's start with what happened to you and how you are feeling about it."

****

CHAPTER
FORTY-SIX

RACHEL WAS FINISHING HER LAST class for the day. She had been making significant progress in all her classes during the current semester. She had mistakenly left her phone at home, so she couldn't find out if she was scheduled to work her part-time job later. She walked home enjoying the day. However, she had an odd feeling she couldn't shake. When she got home, she had three unheard messages. The first one was from her part-time job telling her she was scheduled to work. The second one was from the leader of her study group. He was giving her possible dates and times for their next session. The third one was very disturbing. She had to listen to it three times to make sure she completely understood it. Her mother's voice was faint, and she didn't speak in complete sentences. When she was sure she'd captured everything her mother said, she called Northwestern Hospital, talked to one of the nurses on her mother's floor, and immediately took an Uber to the hospital. On the way, she called her job and told them she would not be coming to work.

"I'm sorry, but she went into cardiac arrest. She is still in the ICU. We are not sure what the cause was. It had happened three other times since she's been here. If you want to know more about her condition, the doctor will be on the floor in about thirty minutes. You can sit right over there until he comes."

Rachel saw five or six chairs lined up against the wall. She walked over, sat down, and started to ponder all she'd heard from the nurse. *"Cardiac arrest four times, in ICU, not sure about her condition. Will I be able to see her, to talk to her? Is she likely to recover? We haven't had the best relationship since she's been out of prison. I was the one who told her to find her own place and move out of my apartment. But I didn't wish her any ill will. Lord, I pray you would heal and restore her."*

Just then, she realized someone was standing close to her. She looked up as the person asked, "Are you Rachel Frazier?"

"Yes, I am."

"I'm Dr. Thomas. I have been the one responsible for your mother's care since she was brought here after the car accident."

"Doctor, thank you for coming to talk to me. What can you tell me about all of this?"

The doctor sat next to her and told her all he knew about what happened to her mother, from her being hit by the SUV to her currently being in ICU.

When he finished, Rachel appreciated that he waited for her to respond. She said, "What should I expect at this point?"

"Honestly, we aren't sure. When she regains consciousness, we will have a better idea. I would suggest you stay close by because it may be your only time to communicate with her."

"I see."

"Do you have any more questions?"

"No. But thank you for talking to me."

"If you need anything, the nurses will be able to help you. And if you need to talk to me again, have the nurses page me."

"Great, thank you so much."

"Oh, one question...does your mother have any healthcare coverage? All of her care will need to be paid for at some point."

"I don't know, but I will try and find out."

"Fine, I have to go. I wish you and your mother the best."

"Thanks."

With his last comment, he turned, walked to the nurse's station, talked for a minute, and then disappeared down the hall. Once again, Rachel was left alone with her thoughts.

CHAPTER
FORTY-SEVEN

JACK SAT ALONE IN HIS home office. Gloria had gone out to an appointment. He was greatly perplexed. The last three days had been a tornado of events. The press had produced an onslaught of negative articles and news reports regarding Jack, the Feds' ongoing inquiry, the company's falling stock price, and the speculations that Universal was being sold. It seemed everywhere he turned there was more bad news. He felt a degree of safety in his home because he knew Arnie was in his family room. Arnie had checked out the license plates on the car from the night the two of them had been attacked. His contacts in Homeland Security were still trying to determine who the car belonged to. Arnie did determine the regular limousine driver, Ricky, had called in sick the day he was supposed to pick up Jack and Arnie. His replacement was a brand-new guy who apparently had been thoroughly checked out. But he had mysteriously disappeared after the incident at the airport.

Jack had talked to his confidants and mentors. Yet, he still didn't have a clear sense of what he should do regarding the sale offer. He was told by the Board and by OMS he needed to provide an answer, or the decision would be taken out of his hands, and it would be left to the shareholders to decide. In addition, Clarence was still waiting for his case to be heard. Because of the efforts of his boss, the hearing was postponed. So, for Jack, everything was up in the air. He needed a clear solution before things started crashing down on him.

Amid his ruminations, the front doorbell rang. Since his home office was closer to the front door than the den where Arnie was, Jack walked to the door and looked through the peephole. He saw a guy in a delivery uniform holding a package and a clipboard. He opened the door and the guy said, "I have a special delivery package for a Mr. Jack Alexander."

Without thinking, Jack took the package and the guy said, "Please sign here next to your name." Jack took the pen, signed his name, thanked the guy, and closed the door.

Arnie called out from the den in the back of the house, "Who was at the door?"

Jack responded, "I just got a special delivery package. It probably came from the office."

Instinctively, Arnie asked as he looked out of a side window, "Were you expecting anything?" Before Jack could answer, Arnie saw a man in a delivery uniform walking at a rapid pace down the street. He ran to Jack, tore the package from him, opened the front door, sprinted to the street, put the package down, turned, and scampered behind a truck parked at the curb. Just before he was completely hunkered down, he heard an ear-splitting explosion. He waited a full minute before moving to the side of the truck. Debris covered the street and the sidewalks.

He stood up, walked to the street, and began examining the remains from the blast. He was looking for something which would indicate the timing device used and anything else about the bomb. From his experience in Afghanistan, he knew what to look for. He took a handkerchief from his pocket and picked up some items off the ground.

Satisfied with what he found, he went back to Jack's house. Jack was standing inside the house. It was clear he was extremely shaken up.

As Arnie came through the front door, he looked at Jack who said, "A bomb, a bomb...someone planted a bomb in a package addressed to me?" What is this all about? Why would anyone want to send a bomb to my house?"

Arnie put his arm around Jack, led him to a chair and sat him in it. For several minutes, neither of them said anything. Finally, Arnie spoke. "Did you get a good look at the guy? How tall was he, what color hair, was he heavy-set, did he have any tattoos or body markings?" He realized Jack was still in shock. He added, "Look, Jack you may be having a difficult time right now. However, this is the best time to try and remember whatever you can since it is still fresh in your mind." He could see Jack was thinking through the questions.

Finally, Jack said, "He was medium height, five foot nine or so, he had sandy brown hair. I would guess he was about one hundred and eighty pounds. Based on the way he held the package, the clipboard, and the pen, he was left-handed. Other than those things, I don't remember anything else about him."

He made mental notes of the things Jack said. He was about to say something else when Jack blurted out, "Oh, he had a pierced earring on his left ear."

He noticed Jack had settled down considerably. Thinking about the answers to Arnie's questions had cause him to focus on something other than the bomb and the explosion. However, Arnie was upset because he had allowed the situation to happen. He let his guard down for an instant and it almost cost Jack's life. When the doorbell rang, Arnie should have made a beeline to the front door. Instead, he had hesitated, and he and his client were facing the consequences. Arnie decided right then, *"From now on, my senses will be on red alert. I will be out front of every possible situation."*

FORTY-EIGHT

RACHEL CALLED HER SCHOOL, HER work, and her closest friends. She told them her situation. Everyone was deeply moved and asked to help in any way they could.

The hospital staff found a cot and allowed her to sleep in an area close to the ICU. She had been there for twelve hours and nothing about her mom's condition had changed. Rachel's eyes had closed from fatigue and exhaustion when a nurse touched her shoulder. Rachel opened her eyes and sat straight up.

"What? What's happened?"

"Rachel, I'm sorry to startle you. Your mother regained consciousness about fifteen minutes ago. The doctor said it would be okay for you to go in and talk to her. We're not sure how much time she has. Her condition has actually worsened."

"Worsened…what does that even mean? The doctor's description of her condition was bad. Now you are telling me her condition has gone from bad to worse."

"Yes, that's right. But, if I were you, I wouldn't stand on ceremony right now. My suggestion is you go in and visit with your mother. Talk to her about whatever is on your mind and your heart. We just don't know how long she has."

Rachel got up off the cot, spent a minute in the bathroom, and then followed the nurse to the ICU. After donning a gown and gloves, she went to her mother's bedside. Rachel was shocked at how frail and anemic her mother looked. She also saw all the tubes and monitors she was attached to. She was surprised at how small her mother seemed. Her eyes were closed, and it was clear she was having a difficult time breathing. Tears welled up in Rachel's eyes. This was her mother who was lying before her struggling to live. She noticed her mother's eyes fluttering. She kept intently watching her. Her eyes opened fully and then Rachel realized her mother was trying to speak. It was hard to hear her or try to figure out what she was saying.

Rachel moved close to her bedside, leaned over, and got to the point where their heads were almost touching. Then she heard, "…so, I really screwed up this time. I thought I had it all figured out, but it all backfired."

She stopped talking, but Rachel was perplexed by what she heard. "Mom, what are you saying? What are you trying to tell me? Should I call for the doctor?"

She watched her mother shake her head, raise one of her frail hands, and motion for Rachel to come even closer. Then she started talking again, "I need to right all the wrongs I've done. I have to set it all straight before it's too late."

"Mom, settle what? What wrongs are you talking about?"

Now the tears in Rachel's eyes started flowing again. They were falling from her eyes to her mother's bed sheets. She decided her mother was delusional from her condition and the medication she was on. At that moment, her mother seemed to rally, and her eyes were clear, and her movements were more exact. In her still unsteady condition, she said, "Rachel, go get a pen and paper. I need to tell you some things and you need to write down exactly what I tell you."

Rachel wasn't sure she should go anywhere. She was determined to stay with her mother. The nurse walked in to see how she was doing. Rachel asked her, "Could you please get me a pen and paper to write on? It's important."

The nurse quickly disappeared, then came back with what Rachel requested. She thanked her and turned back to her mother. "Mom, I've got what you asked for. What did you need me to write?"

With her renewed energy, her mother spoke. "First, tell the nurse to stay. I need her to witness what I'm telling you."

Rachel turned to the nurse who nodded.

"Okay, the nurse is here. Go on with what you want to tell me."

With even more clarity than Rachel had previously seen from her mother, Catherine started talking in a clear but raspy voice. "Do you remember Mr. Jack Alexander?"

Rachel's eyebrows went up as she was surprised by the name. But she tried to keep her voice calm. "Yes Mom, I remember him. What does he have to do with anything?"

"I have been angry with him all these years. I have been committed to taking him down."

"Taking him down! What does that even mean?"

"Rachel, please, I need you to be quiet, listen, and write."

"Fine, I'm listening."

"I got involved with some bad people whose sole purpose has been to buy the company where Jack Alexander works. I helped them create a scheme to get Universal Systems to sell their company to them. I did it because I wanted to hurt and ridicule him. But since I've been in the hospital, I've come to realize how wrong I have been. I've been harboring anger and vengeance toward this man for too long."

Rachel could hear her mom's voice starting to fade. Her eyes were closing, and her head fell back on her pillow. So, she said, "Mom, I get it. You are remorseful and you want me to know it. Now you should rest and conserve your strength."

She saw her mom wave her hand at her. She responded in a groggy voice, "I told you to be quiet, listen to me, and write! I need to stop these people before it's too late. I recorded all the conversations I had with them. I also have documents and payment records. I need you to get together everything and take it to the authorities immediately."

Rachel wrote down every word her mother said. She wanted to be sure not to miss anything. When she was sure her mother was finished, she asked, "I understood everything you said, I wrote down your instructions, but where do I find all these documents and recordings?"

She couldn't tell if her mother had fallen asleep or was even conscious. She wasn't moving and her eyes were closed. She turned to the nurse as if asking for her opinion.

Just as she turned away, her mother started speaking in a raspy-sounding voice. "Did you get all that?"

A bit shocked and startled, Rachel looked back at her mother and said, "Yes, Mom, I got everything you said. But where do I find the stuff to give to the authorities?"

"In my purse there is a safe deposit key. It has the number 370918 on it."

"Yes, but I can't go to a bank and get things from your safe deposit box..."

Rachel was surprised by how forceful her mother's reaction was.

"How many times do I need to tell you to be quiet, listen, and write?"

Rachel didn't apologize. She sat still, kept her pen poised, and waited for her mother's next words.

"I wasn't sure if I would ever need to use the documents. But I figured if something happened to me, you would be the only person to help me. You are the only other person who can gain access to the box. Your ID and the key are the only things you'll need. Understand?"

Rachel was not sure if she should reply. But in a weak, timid voice she said, "Yes, I understand."

She continued to sit there with the nurse behind her, holding her pen, and waiting for her mother to speak. After a prolonged silence, her mother turned, looked in Rachel's direction, and in a hoarse voice said,

"Why are you still sitting here? You don't have a moment to lose. These people are going to make some bad stuff happen unless you get moving right now."

"Okay, Mom, I'm on my way."

FORTY-NINE

"**YOUNG LADY, I WILL NEED** some identification."

Rachel opened her purse, took out her driver's license and her student ID card with her picture on it, and handed then to the person behind the desk at Chase Bank.

The woman examined Rachel's identification, handed them back to her, and said, "I can take you to the safe deposit box now."

Rachel followed the woman down a flight of stairs, stood behind her as the woman said something to another bank person, and then walked in as the door to the safe deposit section opened. Rachel was escorted to the box; she used her key to open it, and then she was shown to a room. They closed the door.

Rachel sat down and stared at the box without moving. She thought, *"Well, I'm here. I can't back out now. I promised my mom I would go through with this."* She mustered up the courage to open the box. To her surprise, there were very few things in it. She found a 3-ring spiral notebook, some papers, and three CDs. She looked at the papers, perused through the notebook, and studied the labels on the CDs. None of what she saw or read made any sense to her. She took the contents and put them in her purse. She leaned back in her chair and determined what she would do next. Her mother told her to take the contents to the authorities, but Rachel wasn't sure who she should go see.

As she sat there pondering her next move, she remembered when she saw Jack Alexander get kidnapped in a parking garage years ago. She recalled going to the Chicago Police Department. They assigned her to an officer. She closed her eyes and thought, *"what was his name? Think, think…you've got to remember! Was his name Michaels, MacDonald, McMillian? No, no, it was McClain. That's right, it was McClain. I'll go see Officer, Detective, or Sergeant McClain. He'll know what to do. Hopefully, he'll remember me. Oh…I don't know if that's a good thing or a bad thing."*

****

The Uber driver knew exactly where the police station was. As Rachel got out of the car and looked at the building, memories from past events involving the police, her mother, and Jack Alexander flooded her mind. She reflected on them as she walked into the building. None of her recollections were pleasant. She realized she had come too far to turn around and leave because she had promised her mother, who was likely dying.

As she approached the policewoman at the desk, she heard, "Ma'am, how can I help you?"

"I'm here to talk to Officer McClain."

Rachel could tell the policewoman had a strange look on her face and asked, "You mean Lieutenant McClain?"

Rachel thought for a few seconds. *"I guess it has been years since I saw him. He probably got promoted."*

She replied, "Yes, yes…I mean Lieutenant McClain."

"What is this concerning? Do you know him personally? Are you a relative?"

"This is a matter of grave urgency. And, yes, I know him personally. My name is Rachel Frazier. My mother is Catherine Frazier. If you tell him I am here, I am certain he will want to see me."

Rachel could see the desk sergeant was looking at her with one eyebrow raised above the other. She had a smirk on her face that portrayed disbelief as she picked up the phone and dialed a number. She said something to the person who answered. She listened, hung up, and said to Rachel, "Have a seat over there. Someone will come down to talk to you."

What she heard didn't sound promising. But, she turned, walked over to a row of plastic chairs bolted to the floor, and sat down. More than twenty minutes passed, and she was beginning to feel she had made a mistake. She looked up at an older, grayer, and heavier version of McClain. He had stopped in front of her and said, "Rachel Frazier…what brings you to the Chicago Police Department? Did somebody else get kidnapped?"

Rachel gave him a half smile at his attempt at humor. She collected her things, stood, and said, "Sir, I have a very grave situation and I need your help. Time is of the essence. Based on what I know, we don't have a moment to lose."

McClain stood there collecting his thoughts, then said, "Young lady, follow me."

Rachel was surprised when he turned, started walking back in the direction he had come, opened a door with his key, stood back, allowed Rachel to walk ahead, and then locked the door behind him.

They were standing in a small interrogation room. It had a small table and two chairs. McClain said, "Take a seat and tell me what's going on."

For the next twenty minutes, Rachel shared with him the situation. When she finished, she watched him stand up, walk to the door, and say, "Wait here, I'll be back."

Rachel waited for ten minutes before the door reopened. McClain came back with a CD player. He put it on the table, took one of the CDs, and loaded it in the device. They waited for a couple seconds before the CD player came to life. They sat and listened to multiple conversations. Eventually, McClain hit the Pause button. He turned to Rachel. "Have you ever heard any of this before?"

"No…I got all of these items from my mother's safe deposit box, immediately took an Uber here, and asked for you."

"You did the right thing."

For the first time, Rachel relaxed. She could see she'd made the right decision by coming to him for help. She watched McClain pull out his cell phone, dial some numbers, and start speaking in low tones. She couldn't figure out what he was saying, but it was clear he was taking everything serious. After a few minutes of talking, she saw him put his phone on the table, look in the 3-ring binder, and then stare off into space.

Rachel was just left waiting until he said, "How's your mother?"

"Honestly, I don't know. She was in bad shape when I left the hospital. The medical staff doesn't know how long she has left to live."

"So, we can't talk to her?"

"I would say, No! She gave me instructions to get all this"—she waved her hand over the items on the table—"to the authorities so you could stop the bad guys."

She expected him to say something, but McClain didn't say anything. He was deep in thought. Then Rachel watched him jump up and say, "Okay, let's go!"

She saw him collect all the items on the table into a bag marked Evidence, pick up his phone, and start to walk out the door with her in tow.

"**I**'M SORRY, I THOUGHT THIS was the number for Special Agent Harper. Did I misdial?"

"No, you didn't dial the wrong number. Special Agent Harper is on an extended leave of absence. Can I help you with something?"

"I'm not sure. Who am I speaking to?"

"I can answer that question when I know who's calling the FBI on an agent's special phone number."

"Oh right...I'm Lieutenant McClain from the Chicago Police department. Special Agent Harper and I worked together on a kidnapping case a few years back."

"Okay, but why are you trying to reach him now?"

"Right...great question. Now I've told you who I am, but I don't know who I'm speaking to."

"Fair enough, I am Harry Coombs, supervisor of Special Agent Harper. So, now we got all the formalities out of the way, I still don't know why you are calling the FBI."

McClain thought about how to answer, then he said, "Fair question…some vitally important information has been brought to my attention. The information has to do with the victim in the kidnapping case I mentioned."

"Okay, so I'll bite, who was this victim?"

"A guy by the name of Jack Alexander."

There was silence on the line for an inordinate period. McClain eventually said, "Are you still there?"

"How quickly can you get to our FBI offices? And can you bring the information you mentioned with you."

"Uh, with traffic, I can be there in twenty minutes."

"Fine, ask for me when you arrive, and I'll come out and get you."

McClain didn't immediately respond. Coombs said, "Are we clear? Is there a problem, Lieutenant?"

McClain spoke up. "I need to bring the person who brought the information to me. She is vital and germane to this whole thing."

"Fine, if Agent Harper worked with you, I trust your judgement. Bring her with you. By the way, what's her name?"

"Rachel Frazier."

"Great, I'll expect you in twenty minutes."

****

After Harry Coombs reviewed the written information and listened to the CDs, he began questioning Rachel. "So, your mother was deeply involved with these people until she was hit by a car a few days ago?"

"Yes, sir."

"Rachel, please pardon me for being so morose, but your mother, Catherine Frazier, gave you her deathbed confession at Northwestern Hospital?"

"Yes, sir."

"Did anyone else hear what your mother told you?"

"Yes, the nurse who's been caring for my mother."

"Please forgive me for asking in such a direct way, but is your mother still alive?"

"Yes…just barely. I called the hospital earlier today and the nurse told me she is hanging on by a thread."

"Young lady, I'm sorry to hear that. I hope she recovers."

Rachel gave no reply. She just looked down at her folded hands resting on the table. Eventually, she looked up at the two men in the room. Her eyes were filled with tears. Then she choked out the words, "My mother asked me to get this information to the proper authorities so these evil people could be stopped. Her wish was that these people would not complete their dishonest deeds and wreck innocent people's lives. I want to know if you are going to make her wish, maybe her dying wish, come true?"

Harry was the first to speak. "With the information, recordings, and all these details, we have more than enough to bring these people down. Now, we recommend you go and be at your mother's side. Tell her you have fulfilled her wish and the proper authorities are on the case."

"Thank you, I will tell her."

She rose, collected her belongings, and headed towards the door.

Before she opened the door, Harry said, "Ms. Frazier, thank you for bringing all this to light. We appreciate what you have done."

Rachel made a half turn toward them, nodded her head, opened the door, and left the room.

Coombs and McClain stared at each other before McClain said, "We'd better put our game plan together if we are going to stop these clowns."

"What do you suggest?"

"Well, for sure, we need to get in touch with Jack Alexander. He needs to know what is going on and that we are on to this scheme."

"Good point. Hold on to your thought. I need to get some of my agents in here."

Coombs picked up the phone, punched in a few numbers, and waited for someone to answer.

"Hello?"

"Agnes, this is Coombs, I need you to get five or six of my agents in conference room two. Tell them it's a Red Alert. You know who to tell. Thanks."

Coombs looked over at McClain. McClain said, "My guess is that now the heavy lifting starts."

CHAPTER
FIFTY-ONE

"YES, I REALIZE YOU'RE IN the middle of your investigation of both Jack Alexander and Universal. There is some new information that we believe requires your immediate attention."

Harry listened to the response he received. He looked up at the ceiling in utter frustration. Then he said, "No, I believe it can't wait any longer. If we do, we will invoke a huge injustice which may be irreversible. What I need is—"

He was interrupted. He gritted his teeth and clenched his fist. He used patience to calm himself and not yell in the phone. He continued to listen until he heard, "Okay, you've got twenty minutes to tell me what's so important. And you need to be here in exactly fifteen minutes from now."

"Thank you, sir. I will be there in twelve."

Harry hung up the phone, looked around the room at the agents and McClain, gathered up the information, and headed out the door. His only comment was, "If you know how to pray, now would be the time. I'll be back!"

****

Harry had one of his agents waiting for him when he exited the building. He jumped in the car, and they sped down Roosevelt Road above the legal speed limit. Harry kept saying, "Drive, drive, if you have to break some laws to get me there, you have my permission!"

The agent went through at least three red lights. Nine minutes later, he came to a screeching stop in front of 219 South Dearborn, where Assistant Director from the Criminal Division Ralph Martinez's office was located. Harry jumped out of the car, ran to the entrance to the building, showed his identification, hopped in the first available elevator, and got off on the seventh floor. He walked into Martinez's outer office, told the secretary who he was, and got escorted into the Director's office.

Ralph Martinez was sitting behind his desk when Harry came in. He said, "Sir, thank you for seeing me on such short notice. I promise to get right to the point."

"Coombs, I give you credit, you got here with two minutes to spare. So, what's so darn important that couldn't wait until tomorrow?"

"Sir, you and your team, made up of Justice Department and FBI personnel, are looking into bribery charges against Jack Alexander and Universal Systems. We have acquired information you need to know as it has a direct bearing on your inquiry."

Harry watched Martinez shift uncomfortably in his chair, blink several times, and start rubbing his hands. Then he replied, "What...what information?"

"Would you be surprised if I told you there was a plot to incriminate both Special Agent Harper and Jack Alexander of bribery?"

"Incriminate them…why would anyone want to do such a thing?"

"There's a Fortune 500 company at stake."

"What company? Who's involved in this and why?"

For the next thirty minutes the two of them discussed the case. Martinez asked numerous questions, but in the end, he sat and listened. Harry had virtually every answer based on listening to the CDs and reading Catherine Frazier's notes.

Finally, Martinez waved his hand and said, "Stop, stop…I've heard enough. It is clear we were about to do a huge injustice to Universal and Jack Alexander. Knowing what you know now, what do you suggest we do to fix this situation?"

"Sir, we have a plan, and we are ready to deploy it. Here's what we would do."

Harry spent a few more minutes providing the details of the plan. When he finished, he noticed Martinez was uncomfortable. Then he heard him say sheepishly, "It's a great plan. You have my agreement to put it in place immediately. The FBI should be the ones to carry it out. I think we have done enough to murky up the waters on this one. I just hope you aren't too late."

"Sir, thanks. We will be sure to circle back with you."

"Great. Now get out of here and go make it happen!"

"Right!"

CHAPTER
FIFTY-TWO

WHEN RACHEL GOT BACK TO the hospital, she went right to the ICU. She saw the attending nurse walking toward her. Rachel tried to read her facial expression, but she couldn't.

When they were close to each other, the nurse said, "Rachel, it's good to see you. I'm glad you are back."

"What's the status of her condition?"

Rachel watched the nurse look away before she answered, as if she was trying to gather her thoughts. Then she said, "We are not sure how much time she has left. She has been asking for you. So, you should go right in. Later, the doctor can explain her condition and answer any question you have."

Rachel was stunned by what she heard. Her only response was, "Okay."

She started walking slowly to her mother's room. Never in her life had she gone through an end-of-life experience with a loved one. She knew her mother was ailing. Yet, she somehow expected her to recover. As she reached the door, before she turned the doorknob to go in, she said a quiet prayer.

She went in, closed the door, and walked to her mother's bedside. She was not prepared for what she saw. Her mother seemed to have shrunk in size; her skin was ashen, pale gray in color. It seemed she was hooked to even more monitors. Her mother's head was turned away from the door.

As Rachel walked closer to her bedside, her mother said in a weak, groggy voice, "Please go away, I only want to see my daughter."

Rachel was surprised. After all these years, she longed to hear those words from her mother. Rachel got closer to the bed and whispered, "Mom, It's me, Rachel."

Her mother slowly turned her head until they were face-to-face. "Did you take care of all the things I asked you to do? Were the authorities notified? Did you get all of the contents from the safe deposit box?"

Rachel hesitated to make sure she provided a fulsome answer. "Yes, Mom, I did everything you asked of me. I made sure every item on your list was completed."

Rachel watched as her mother's facial features softened; her mouth relaxed, and her eyes closed slightly. She reached out her hand and Rachel took it. Her mother said, "You are a good daughter. You have always sought to be in a relationship with me. On the other hand, I have always had an agenda…,me trying to manipulate you."

Rachel felt her mother's grip tighten. Then she continued, "I'm sorry I wasn't a better mother to you. There was so much more I could have done to enhance the bond between us."

Tears started to form in Rachel's eyes. She couldn't control them as they fell from her eyes to her mother's bedcovers. These were words she had longed to hear. She was speechless.

Her mother continued, "I realized as I lay here, I could not have done all I needed to do without you."

Rachel watched her mother as she, too, had tears in her eyes. Rachel saw them spill down her mother's face. Rachel felt her mother's grip increase. She didn't want the moment to end. She felt she finally had her mother's undiminished love. She closed her eyes and basked in the love her mother was showering on her.

Just at the apex of her feelings, she felt her mother's hand pressure dissipate. She opened her eyes, looked down at her mother, and realized she'd passed away. As the moments passed by, Rachel continued holding her hand. Without trying to wipe them away, she let the tears continue to run down her face. While she was sad because of her mother's departure, she was thankful she got to hear her mother's affirming, loving, last words.

FIFTY-THREE

I T HAD BEEN THREE DAYS since the bomb explosion. Arnie had the debris he'd picked up from the street analyzed. It was determined the bomb was expertly designed to go off two minutes after the detonator was activated. The alleged delivery man probably set off the timer as he walked away from Jack's house. There were no CCTV cameras in the neighborhood. There was no way to determine a description beyond what Jack remembered.

As Arnie drove them to the office, Jack asked, "What did you find out about the bomb?"

Arnie shared what he knew and then added, "Whoever it was wanted to take you out. I'm sorry I wasn't sharp enough to figure out what was happening sooner."

"Are you kidding me? If you hadn't reacted like you did, I may not be alive today."

Arnie let him finish and then said, "Yes, but I shouldn't have let you answer the door without me being there. Nothing like that will happen again."

****

Jack sat in the company's conference room with Arnie, a bunch of FBI agents, and one lieutenant from the Chicago Police department. He was overwhelmed by all the details they described. When he heard Catherine Frazier's name as both perpetrator and whistleblower, he was totally surprised. He remembered Lieutenant McClain as one of the people who had helped rescue him when he got kidnapped years ago. He wasn't sure yet what the FBI's plan was. However, he sensed they had one.

After more than an hour, he understood the elaborate scheme Armando had hatched, the plan the FBI had laid out, and the important role Jack was to play.

Decisively, Coombs asked, "Mr. Alexander, are you clear as to what you are to do and what you need to say?"

"I think so."

"Good! Remember, to pull this off, no one other than you and the people in this room can know about our plan. Are you completely clear?"

"Well, I hope so."

"Look, much of this plan's success depends on you. Again, what time is the final takeover meeting tomorrow?"

"Ten a.m."

"Good. One more time, I want you to follow our instructions to the letter, no deviations."

"I just hope I can pull this off."

****

The sun was setting in the west. He could barely see the last few rays of sunlight rushing to meet the horizon. A vast array of colors warmed his soul every time he saw more elements of the sunset. He felt it was God's reminder of what He had lovingly provided, a foretaste of what He had in store for the next day. Jack felt he was on a sunset quest, realizing it would be dark long before he got home. He strained his neck and turned his head whenever a snatch of sunlight appeared. It lifted his spirits. Though, when he happened to look to the east, the sun's impact on Lake Michigan was nonexistent. The darkness had fallen over the water. The waves, the shoreline, and the eastern horizon were hidden under the obscurity of the night. In addition, far off in the distance, he could see repeated flashes of lightning. There was no way for him to tell if they would invade his tomorrow or stay miles away on the other side of the lake. It wasn't cold in the car, but he began to feel a slight chill. He immediately thought about tomorrow's meeting with Armando. He realized again the outcome of what was to happen was somewhat concealed from his view.

He had almost forgotten about Arnie, who drove along allowing Jack to remain in his thoughts. Eventually, Arnie interrupted the silence. He asked, "You have been quiet the whole trip back. I realize it was a lot to consume this afternoon. Would you like some advice?"

Jack had come to appreciate Arnie and his sage wisdom. He had become much more than a bodyguard. Over a short period of time, he had provided Jack with wise nuggets designed to encourage him.

With things now taking a different turn, it seemed to make sense to hear what he had to say. "Uh huh."

"I remember as a kid the streets were tough. To survive you had to be strong. If the other kids sensed your weakness, they would exploit it. So, I'd sometimes have to 'fake it to make it.' After a while, I got stronger and could take care of myself. Nobody bothered me anymore. But I still had to put on my 'tough face' at times to let everybody know I had no soft spots where they could take advantage of me. I tell you all this to say, you have been pushed and shoved around. There have been times when you weren't sure if you would survive. Now, your change has come. Tomorrow will be the opportunity for you to put on your 'tough guy' face. You'll let the folks from OMS know you are done being pushed around. So, say what you are planning to say with power and conviction."

He thought about what Arnie said. There was truth to his words. He needed to speak boldly tomorrow. After some additional reflection, he said, "I just hope I can do it."

They rode the rest of the way in silence. He was thinking of what he was going to say to Gloria. Arnie dropped him off and they agreed on the pickup time in the morning for the ride to the office.

He walked in the back door and the first thing he heard was, "So, how did it go today, honey?"

He had committed to the FBI he would not tell anyone about the details for the upcoming meeting tomorrow. There was so much riding on what would happen. He didn't want to lie to Gloria, yet he couldn't share any of the particulars with her.

"Babe, my day was fine. Overall, it went well. Yet, I am really glad to get home tonight."

"Well, it's good to have you home. I can tell from the tone of your voice you don't want to talk about what went on today. So, I won't press you. I do want to talk to you about the blinds. Did you remember they are being installed next week? Do you plan to be here?"

Jack was so thankful. He was happy to talk about the blinds; anything but the FBI meeting. He answered, "Yes, honey, I do remember. If you want me to be here, I'm happy to do so."

CHAPTER
FIFTY-FOUR

ARMANDO SAT IN HIS HOME office smiling. He thought, *"This is great! I am hours away from owning Universal Systems. Everything I've orchestrated has come together nicely, no loose ends. Jack Alexander should have known from the start he was no match for me. In some ways, it's hard to believe we will be the dominant force, the largest firm in our industry. My dad never dreamed this would be possible. Nevertheless, it is about to happen. Nothing can stand in our way. I was concerned Catherine Frazier knew too much about all the bribery, extortion, and payoffs we needed to make. Arranging for her to be hit by the SUV was the final capstone. When I had my people place the tracking device in her bag and on her phone, I knew it would eventually come in handy. I never expected her to leave the scene of the accident alive. But she is a tough old bird. I'll have to call in a favor to make sure she never leaves the hospital. So, what will I do first after the last document gets signed and the company is finally in my hands? Okay, okay, okay…I need to keep a level head and my wits about me. I need to get some sleep, so I am well rested for this big extravaganza tomorrow."*

CHAPTER
FIFTY-FIVE

THE NEXT MORNING, ARNIE ARRIVED early at Jack's home. By now, he knew where all the foodstuff and dishes were.

Jack watched as Arnie put together breakfast for them. He was glad he didn't have to wake Gloria who had told him the night before she would cook. Lost in his thoughts, he was reflecting on the upcoming meeting. He felt everything would go according to plan, but he had his doubts. *"What if this whole thing falls apart and the company gets sold after all? What then? A part of me feels like I need to prepare for the worst-case scenario. Wait a minute, this is the FBI. If they flop, all is lost. I need to trust this will all come together."*

Arnie finished cooking breakfast. He stuck a plate under Jack's nose, and they both ate in silence. Ten minutes later, Arnie said, "It's time… we need to leave."

The car ride was a silent one. He was thankful Arnie allowed him space so he could go over the details for the day.

When they were ten minutes from the office, Arnie said, "Hey, man, I know you are nervous and worried about everything. But you need to try and relax, stay calm, and trust the process. Rely on your instincts. The plan we heard yesterday *will work*. There are still some moving parts, but it will all come together."

Jack turned his head, looked at Arnie while he was still talking, and tried to take in his comments. When Arnie finished, Jack said, "I wish I were as confident about the outcome as you are. I'm nervous as a cat on a hot tin roof."

Again, there was extended silence. Without looking at Jack, Arnie said, "Whatever happens today, know I am with you."

****

As Jack sat in his office collecting his notes and other documents, he had a thought. He stopped what he was doing, got up from his desk, walked to his office window, and looked out at Lake Michigan. It was an overcast day. The boats were being tossed about by bigger than usual waves. He started praying. "Father God, you have been faithful to me in every aspect of my life. I do trust you. Today, I need your Divine Intervention in this meeting. I can't see the outcome because of the shrouded covering. Nevertheless, I'm trusting in you. Guide and protect me Lord, in your Son's name, Amen."

There was a peace and calm he felt as he walked back over to his desk, gathered up his papers, and walked to the conference room.

****

"Do you know why Armando wants you there?"

"I guess so he's assured of the Board's full support of this deal going through."

"True. Any other reason?"

"I don't want to sit here and make up stuff. So, why don't you just tell me."

"Do I sense a bit of arrogance in your tone? Need I remind you how important it is for you for this deal to be completed today?"

"No, there is no need to remind me. I am fully aware of the implications. I simply want to know specifically why Armando wants me at the meeting. A simple answer would help me immensely. Everyone knows exactly where I stand on this deal."

"Okay, okay… Armando wants you to run interference in case any issues come up. You need to be the voice of reason and brush back any potential concerns."

"Got it! But I don't envision anything popping up. As far as I'm concerned, this is a done deal."

"Exactly how we see it. However, he likes to cover all possible contingencies. If it's required, that's where you come in."

"Okay. Anything else?"

"Nope, now that I am sure we are on the same page. I'll let him know about our little talk and I'll see you at the meeting."

"Right!"

CHAPTER
FIFTY-SIX

J ACK HIT THE INTERCOM AND Beth picked up.

"Beth, please walk in here for a moment."

When she came in, Jack immediately said, "I'm so sorry... I meant to ask you to do this yesterday. For our meeting with the OMS folks, I want you to reserve the large conference room down on the first floor. If someone has already reserved it, tell them they are being preempted and they can use my regular conference room. Be sure to let Tom, Matthew, and Shane know about the change. Since you will be escorting the OMS people, you will know where to bring them."

"No problem, I will take care of it."

****

As Jack pushed open the conference room door, he looked around at the attendees in the room. Tom Wallace and Matthew Warren sat together on one side of the conference room table. Shane McCarthy, the board chairman, sat on the same side of the table, but he separated himself by two chairs. Arnie was standing. It was clear he wouldn't sit until Jack sat down.

Following his predetermined script, Jack said, "Thank you all for being prompt. You all know why we're here. We'll get started as soon as the OMS folks arrive."

Almost as soon as he finished, Armando and Javier walked into the conference room. Armando walked over to Jack and said, as he shook his hand, "Good to see you. I'm ready to finalize this transaction if you are."

Jack looked him in the eyes and replied, "I'm ready to finalize everything we need to do here today."

He watched Armando's eyes. He squinted slightly as if to suggest he wasn't totally sure what Jack's comment meant. Without saying any more, Jack made his way to the head of the table, sat, and Arnie sat to his immediate right. Armando and Javier had already seated themselves opposite Tom and Matthew. It was clear they had expected Jack to sit with his people.

With nothing else said, Jack called the meeting to order. "Armando, thank you for coming here today. I fully understand your reason for being here and what you hope to get out of today's session."

He paused to look at everyone, especially Armando, and let his comments sink in before continuing. "Before we go any further, I have some questions for you, Armando."

He could see Armando's eyebrows go up, expressing his surprise. He looked quickly at Shane and then back at Jack. Nonetheless, he masked his alarm. His voice quivered slightly as he asked, "What questions? I was under the impression we had addressed everything."

"Yes, yes, but humor me. I do have a few questions."

"Okay, ask me. I'm sure I can answer them for you,"

Jack smiled as he quickly went over his predetermined questions in his mind. "Great. Why is it you want to buy Universal Systems?"

"At this point in the acquisition stage, you're asking me a really odd question. Why do you want to know?"

"Trust me, I'm not trying to be ludicrous. But please just answer the question."

Jack observed him squirm in his chair ever so slightly. He even picked up his pen and started lightly tapping on his notepad. Then he said, "In our strategic plan, it has always been our intention to be the leader in our industry. The acquisition of Universal Systems will help us achieve this goal."

"Yes, yes, but why do *you* personally want to buy the company?"

He could tell Armando was increasingly uncomfortable. His eyes started shifting from side to side and he squinted them with a look of disdain. He blurted out, "Where are you going with this? I was under the impression today's meeting was to simply wrap up the negotiations and sign the final transfer documents. If this is some sort of stall tactic, we have ways of dealing with this... Your choice."

He could tell from Armando's manner and tone of voice that he was disturbed and angry. For the first time, Jack could see the veins in his neck bulging out and he increased the tapping of his pen on his notepad. Despite all these signs, he pressed on.

"Trust me, this is not a stall tactic at all. I sense this will likely be the last time we will be together once we are finished here. So, I do have some questions I need to ask for my own satisfaction."

He could see Armando start to relax. He put his pen down and leaned back in his chair. Then he replied, "I see. Well, from the first time I started working for my father in the company, I had a vision of the firm growing to be the largest in this business. So, I have been on this quest ever since."

"Very ambitious goal, and I see your expedition has kept you planning and scheming."

"Yes, in fact, it has."

"Actually, the average person would be a bit envious of you and your purpose-driven life. I can't think of many people who have been as focused on their business career."

He could tell his last comment put a smile on Armando's face. So, he felt it was the right moment to reel him in. So, Jack offered, "I imagine you might consider doing *anything* to make your vision, your dream, a reality?"

Now Jack could sense the confidence and the arrogance rising in Armando just by the way he tilted his head back in a rather mocking fashion. It was evident in his next comment. "I have always been willing to do the things required to make dreams a reality, things others don't either have the stomach or the capacity to do."

It was obvious to Jack he was on a roll. So, he simply smiled and let him continue.

"I have an expression: *Amateurs compete, Professionals create.* It has served me well."

With his comment, Jack proceeded to drop the bomb on him. He replied with, "So, let me get this straight, was it your creativity to hire people to disable Len Shapiro's car which almost cost him his life?"

As soon as he made the comment, three guys walked into the conference room. Two of them had handcuffs on and it was clear the third was an FBI agent. They stood in a place where Armando had to see them. Jack could see Armando's eyes get big and his pupils start dilating. No words came out of his mouth, but it was clear he was surprised. Jack continued, "Was it the same creativity you used to bribe an FBI agent to lie about Special Agent Harper sexually assaulting her?"

Three more people walked into the room. There was a man and a woman who were handcuffed with an agent behind them. They, too, stood in a place where Armando was forced to look at them.

Jack went on. "Did you use your inner capacity to bribe people to create a false money trail between me and Special Agent Harper? And I guess you used your creativity to provide an anonymous tip to the FBI about the same bogus money trail?"

Two women stepped into the room. One was in cuffs and the other a federal agent. They were positioned close to the others.

"Your creativity was certainly at work when you bribed reporters to plant fake news regarding a scenario you and your cronies created."

Three more men appeared in the room, two in handcuffs and one an agent. Jack could see Armando was biting the inside of his mouth. His eyes looked as if they would pop out of his head.

Jack was definitely on a roll now. He said, "And, finally, your creative skills were certainly at work to have Javier here bribe and extort our Board Chairman, Shane, over there, to help manipulate the board in your attempt to take over Universal Systems? Have I, by chance, left anything out?"

Arnie looked at Jack, didn't say a word, but held up four fingers.

It caused Jack to make a final comment. "Oh, yes, how could I forget. You obviously had the stomach to arrange four separate occasions where you sent your goons to threaten my life. I especially took exception to the bomb you had delivered to my home which almost cost me my life."

Just as he finished, five more people walked into the room, three men in hand cuffs and two agents.

There was complete silence in the room. He could have heard a pin drop. He looked around at every person. Both Tom and Matthew had looks of astonishment. Their mouths gaped wide open. Shane was in a crouched position in his chair. His back was hunched over, and his eyes were looking down at his hands which were buried in his lap. Javier tried to give the impression he was taking notes, while trying his best not to look at anyone in the room, including his boss.

Lastly, Jack looked back at Armando and broke the silence. "So, what do you have to say, my friend? Do you no longer have the stomach or the capacity to respond? Now where is your bravado, your machismo?"

He watched Armando as he started to squirm in his chair. His eyes were shooting daggers in Jack's direction. His teeth were clenched, and yet he didn't utter a word. Jack decided to continue. "You have done some detestable things in your attempt to *make your vision come true*. I'm angry at you for all the hurt you've caused. And if it hadn't been for the *deathbed confession* of Catherine Frazier, we would be none the wiser."

As soon as he finished, two men stepped into the conference room. Special FBI Agent Coombs spoke as he stood behind Armando and said, "Armando Santos, you are under arrest for multiple offenses."

Jack was surprised at how Armando suddenly found his voice and replied, "Excuse me, you obviously don't know who I am."

"Did I stutter? I suggest you stand up and comply or my agents will drag you out of here in handcuffs."

Jack could tell from Armando's facial expression he didn't like being told what to do. He had a scowl on his face, his teeth were clenched, and his eyes started to twitch. But slowly, he stood up, turned, and faced Agent Coombs, and said, "I need to call my lawyer,"

"You will have plenty of time to reach your attorney. In the meantime, you have the right to remain silent. Anything you say can and will be used against you in a court of law…"

The same Miranda rights were read to Javier as well. Then Jack watched as Armando and Javier were led out of the conference room. It took a while for all the arrested people and agents to walk out of the large conference room. No one left in the room spoke for a while.

Then Jack looked over at Shane and said, "What you did and what you conspired to do were egregious acts on your part. You were complicit in the awful things Armando instituted. I don't know if the FBI will want you for questioning. Nevertheless, I expect your immediate letter of resignation from the Board. Any and everything you have in your possession associated with Universal Systems; I expect you to return at once to Tom. In addition, effective immediately, you will have no conversation with anyone regarding the affairs of this company. If you *in any way* violate this, we will prosecute you to the full extent the law allows. Is this understood?"

He waited while Shane found his voice. He didn't take his eyes off him, waiting for him to speak. Shane spoke just above a whisper. "Yes, I understand."

Jack looked at him with an angry scowl on his face. He could see Shane looking everywhere else but in Jack's direction. He finished by saying, "We have no further use of your services. Please leave."

He watched as Shane slowly gathered his papers, stood, and walked to the door. Before he opened it, Jack saw him turn toward him and say, "Nothing I can say reverses my errors in judgement, yet, I want to say to you I am truly sorry for my part in all this."

He said nothing in reply. He simply stared as Shane opened the door and vanished down the hall.

EPILOGUE

IN LEN'S FAMILY ROOM, JACK and Len sat quietly looking at each other and reflecting on the tribulations they had gone through. Without any words spoken, they were both grateful nothing more severe had transpired.

Jack broke the silence by saying, "I'm glad to know you have recovered. While you are not fully healed, you are well enough to resume your duties as CEO."

"Come on, you're the CEO, and it should probably stay that way. The board has gotten use to not having me there and you've proven you can handle the job."

"Hold on there, you've got to remember our deal. When you asked me to step in, I agreed to be the CEO only temporarily. Len, the board realizes they were influenced by Shane. Once his motivations were uncovered, they all recognized the errors of their ways. They want you back. Also, no one is better in the role than you. We all need your wisdom. The time for your return is now."

He could see Len was touched by his words. His eyes started to glisten, and Jack could see Len's lips start to quiver. It was one of the few times he'd ever seen him get emotional.

Len replied, "I appreciate the words and the support. If you think it is the right move, I will agree to return. But we need to work on a transition. This whole thing caused me to realize we are all vulnerable."

"Absolutely. In the meantime, we need you back as the captain of the ship."

****

"If I had it to do all over again, I would not have made the accusations against Agent Harper. I have always had the highest respect for him as a man, a husband, a father, and an agent. I learned so much from him. To put him in the situation I did was unconscionable. But I was thinking about my brother. I wanted to help him avoid prison time, and this seemed like a way to help him. In the end, I'm not sure I did anything except cause harm to others who didn't deserve it. I am sorry for my actions. The truth is, I am not worthy to be an FBI agent. I am ready to hand in my badge and accept whatever punishment is due me."

Harry Coombs, Supervisor of both Agent Carla Landers and Agent Clarence Harper, sat at a conference room table with three others. The two women and one man represented a team of experienced lawyers in the FBI's Office of Professional Responsibility. Their role was to determine whether applicable policies, rules, regulations, laws, or other legal standards were violated, and, if so, what penalty should be imposed on the employee in question—up to and including dismissal or imprisonment. Since both agents reported to Harry, he was asked to sit in on the proceedings.

One of the women lawyers, Agent Hudson, responded, "Agent Landers, sexual harassment charges are taken seriously here at the Bureau. And the OPR investigates every claim. For us to now find out your charges were not true and baseless is a problem. It speaks to your lack of integrity as an agent of the FBI."

She stopped for a minute to review her notes. She continued, "Special Agent Harper is one of the best agents we have in the Bureau. We desire more of our agents to follow his example for honesty and incorruptibility. You are correct, you called into question his good name. However, once we understood the underlying issues of your case, it gave us a clearer perspective of the situation. Yet, it doesn't change the reality of what you did. At this point, we are not sure the penalties that should be imposed on you. We will reconvene in fourteen days and inform you as to our final adjudication of misconduct. What we ultimately decide will be reported to the Office of the Inspector General. That will be all. Should we need anything from you before we reconvene, you will be notified. In the meantime, you will be put on administrative leave. This inquiry is adjourned."

Harry watched Agent Landers gather her belongings and walk out. He felt sorry for her, but there was nothing he could do to intervene.

****

"Honestly, they didn't want you to potentially come to my rescue like you did before when I got kidnapped. And the only reason the FBI knew anything about it was due to Catherine Frazier's involvement in their little plot to take over Universal Systems."

Jack looked at Clarence and he sensed mixed emotions. He was smiling, but there was a kind of sadness in his eyes. The last time he saw the same look in Clarence's eyes was when his mother died. He had been out of the country and couldn't get back in time to see her before she passed away. His eyes then reflected a look of helplessness. It was the same look Jack saw now.

Jack continued, "I feel awful for all this being put on you without you being able to defend yourself. If it hadn't been for your boss, Harry Coombs, and Catherine Frazier, I'm not sure how this whole mess would have been resolved."

"Thank you for trying everything you could do to help me. You pulled out all the stops. Actually, you have the makings of a really good FBI agent. If you get tired of working in Corporate America, I think we can find you a role with me in the Bureau."

They both laughed.

****

"Is it all over now? Have the dark clouds passed? Can you tell me the gory details now?"

"Well, yes, the bad stuff has gone away. And, yes, I can tell you the specifics now."

So, Jack spent the next hour sharing with Gloria all of what happened and why he was not at liberty to confide in her earlier.

She asked tons of questions and Jack answered every one of them. In the end, she was relieved. She said, "So much of this I had either figured out or had my suspicions. You've been in some hot spots in the past, but never with people as devious as this Armando character. He seriously wanted Universal Systems at all costs."

Jack smiled at her, knowing she spoke the truth.

****

The room was full of people who had a vested interest in Universal Systems and Jack Alexander. Arnie, Len Shapiro, Tom Wallace, Matthew Warren, Special Agent Harry Coombs, Agent Harper, Lieutenant McClain, Beth Samuels, and Rachel Frazier.

There had been many discoveries over the past few months. The Feds and the FBI slowly unraveled the conspiracy Armando Santos had attempted to orchestrate, the bribery fabrication between Jack and Agent Harper, the attempt on Len Shapiro's life, the multiple attacks on Jack, the blackmailing of FBI Agent Landers, bribing Shane McCarthy to convince the board to dump Len, hire Jack and sell Universal, planting false accusations in the media about Jack, and attempting to cause the market to sell off Universal stock to dramatically lower the company's purchase price. It all would have worked if not for the detailed documentation Rachel obtained from Catherine Frazier's safe deposit box along with Catherine's deathbed confession. In addition, the FBI and the Chicago Police found the people who were hired to hit Catherine with the SUV. As a result of interrogating them, they confessed that Armando was behind this as well.

The Feds had dropped their investigation into the charges against Jack and Agent Harper. The media retracted every inaccurate story and fired the reporters responsible for the egregious acts. The company's stock rebounded to the highest levels in the firm's history. In the end, Armando and a host of his henchmen were brought up on state and federal charges. While the Feds at the table could not talk about the trial since it was still an open investigation, they were smiling and engaged in conversation just the same.

As Jack looked around the room, he was thankful everything had gone according to plan. Armando had no idea he had been found out. Jack was told by a reliable source Armando didn't spend any time in a jail cell, because his attorney arrived at the Midwest FBI offices and posted the required bail. He'd also been told Armando's father was highly incensed when he was informed of the events and immediately took back the reins of the company from his son. One of the first things he did was send a personal apology to Jack.

Jack stood up, put his fingertips on the table, and simply waited until the chatter in the room stopped. Then he said, "Thank you all for coming. I appreciate everything you contributed to the outcome and reversal of what would have been a real travesty. Each of you played a significant role. Yet, the person who made such a huge contribution is not with us today."

Jack stopped and looked at Rachel. His face softened as there was a slight sparkle in his eyes and his lips turned into a big smile. He added, "Rachel, I realize your mother strongly disliked me for several years. Without going through all the details, everyone here is aware she had a change of heart. Her actions helped to save a company and the lives of several people. We owe her enormous debt of gratitude. I asked you here to say, on behalf of Universal Systems and every person in this room, we are thankful for your mother's efforts. And we are deeply sorry for your loss. It was our decision to present you with this check to cover all of her hospital bills, burial expenses, and whatever is left is for you do with it as you see fit."

Jack could see Rachel's eyes fill as she accepted the envelope Jack handed her. When the tears fell down her face, she tried unsuccessfully to wipe them away. Then she replied, "Mr. Alexander, thank you for your comments and your generosity. My mother was a caring and loving person. I loved her deeply."

Their eyes met and there was a real sense of appreciation the two shared with each other. Then Jack turned to the others in the room. He realized there was nothing left to say. Yet, he added, "Thank you all."

****

Jack sat in his family den drinking a combination of orange juice and passion fruit over ice. Arnie was drinking the same. Arnie had driven him home at the end of a long day. He sat on his sofa and didn't speak, just looked off into space. He was exhausted but he didn't want Arnie to leave. Gloria had gone to her elderly parents' home, and he had no idea when she would be back. Neither of them said anything, they just sat. The only sound was the ice moving in their glasses.

Finally, he looked over at Arnie and said, "Thank you again. I couldn't have gotten through all this without you. I am truly indebted to you for all you've done."

He watched Arnie smile and say, "Well, you paid me enough. Good help doesn't come cheap."

"Seriously, all joking aside, you did things for me I couldn't have done for myself. I owe you much more than whatever you were paid. I trusted you with my life and I am grateful."

Jack could now tell whenever Arnie got serious. His voice lowered, his fists were slightly clenched, and he looked right at Jack without blinking. "It was an honor to have worked with you. In my assignments, I've worked with many people. As I told you, I make a policy of not getting too attached to them. But with you, I came to appreciate you, almost like a brother. Once I realized what you were up against, I wanted you to succeed."

Jack hadn't anticipated what he heard from Arnie. But he knew exactly what he meant. He proceeded to say, "Well, I owe you my life. I won't soon forget how you saved me from harm at the tollway plaza or during the bomb scare."

Arnie stood up and said, "Look, I've got to go. Why don't you have Beth set up a time for us to have lunch soon?"

"Great idea. I like that. I'll have her reach out to you. Thanks again, my friend."

He walked Arnie to the front door, opened it, stuck out his hand, and Arnie reached for it with his own. Then they hugged each other. Without saying another word, Arnie turned and walked to his car. He opened the door, got in, and waved as he drove off.

He watched Arnie's car disappear at the next intersection. As he started walking back inside the door, his cell phone buzzed. He looked to see who it was and what the message was.

It was from Michele Thompson,

> **Jack, you asked me to put the financials together with Matthew. I emailed the full report to your private address. Nonetheless, I wanted you to know JPC will end the year at 205% of last year's revenue and an increased profit of 61%. So, you should be ecstatic about exceeding your plan.**

Jack turned his phone off, smiled, and closed his front door.

****

Armando was tried and convicted of several RICO charges. While his henchmen received prison sentences, his were the most severe. He was given 45 to 50 years in the Big Sandy US Penitentiary located in Kentucky.

At the end of the trial, he remained free on bond until he had to surrender to the authorities to begin his sentence. He seriously considered leaving the country and escaping to Columbia, his father's place of origin. It was his father who told him he would be disowned if he fled the country. As a result, he stayed and showed up at his sentence hearing. He listened as the judge said, "Mr. Santos, I have spent a considerable amount of time reviewing your case. I was impressed by the hard work and honesty of your father starting and growing OMS. I read so much about his integrity and how he instilled it in the company. I traced the period when he handed the reins over to you. Two things were clear to me: the company started to grow dramatically and there were incidences of complaints where there had never been any previously. I was shocked by all the crimes you perpetuated in your attempt to acquire Universal Systems. While there were others involved, you were the ringleader. You gave directions to defraud, injure, and kill. You intentionally put in motion a series of events to buy a company through dishonest gain. Therefore, I have decided to punish you with the maximum sentence allowable."

He gazed around his cell which was approximately 6 x 9 x 12 feet. All he had to look at was the bed he was sitting on, a sink, a toilet, and a small picture of his family. As he sat there, he thought, *'I almost pulled it off. If it hadn't been for Catherine Frazier, everything would have gone as planned. Nonetheless, I've got a few more tricks up my sleeve. At some point, I'll be sprung from this place. In the meantime, I'll figure out how I'll get back on top. There is no "quit" in me.'*

THE END

Many of you have been asking, **"Will Jack Alexander be back in the future?"**

Actually, we have been asking ourselves the same question.

SO, LET US KNOW IF YOU WANT "JACK BACK"!!!

Send us a quick email to john@johnwendelladams.com and let us know if you would like to see Jack Alexander return in a new book. The first 100 people to reply will receive a special gift!!!

Please visit us at Our Website: www.johnwendelladams.com

Twitter:http:twitter.com/johnW_Adams@JohnW_Adams

Thank you for buying **Ruthless**. Enjoy it!!!

Also, if you haven't read the first two books in the trilogy, now is a Great Time to buy them. Receive a special deal when you order all three through our website:

Free Shipping on all three books

Reduced price $9.99 on book one "Betrayal" and book two "Payback"

PLEASE GIVE A REVIEW OF THE BOOK ON AMAZON

Go to www.johnwendelladams.com

From the home page, click on the Amazon icon

Scroll down to "Customer Reviews"

Move your cursor over the "5 stars"

Choose and click on the one you want

If you choose to, also write a review

Thank you so much – John Wendell Adams

ACKNOWLEDGEMENTS

There is an old African Proverb, "If you want to go *fast*, go alone. If you want to go *far*, go with others."

TO MY LOVING WIFE GRACE, who continues to be my greatest fan. Her love, support, prayers, and encouragement have been what I needed. Time after time she saw things I couldn't see. She has loved me through this entire process. Thanks, Babe, for all your words inspired by God and your deep love for me.

To my sister Michele who continues to spread the word associated with this labor of love.

To my sister Janet who provided me with helpful tips which added in the book's development.

To Monika Suteski (Monika Suteski Illustration & Design) truly talented designer, who worked diligently to create a compelling book cover despite multiple revisions and changes. Since her efforts with *PayBack*, we have developed a very good working relationship.

To both Burt and Barb who continued to encourage me through the process.

To Mary Harris for another superb editing job. You outdid yourself this time. I received invaluable mentorship from you all along the way. You provided me with critically important suggestions and recommendations which were essential to me as this manuscript evolved. I am a better writer because you challenged me during this process. I believed we would get to the end of this project. Nonetheless, it was more about the journey as you applauded me and cautioned me at various landmarks. You are the Best!

To Lonnie and Pamela who asked repeatedly when the book would be completed.

To Donnie Chambers who made significant comments and recommendations to the character development of both Jack and Catherine throughout the book. He challenged me to determine what they needed to say. I am thankful for his encouragement at critical points along the way.

To my sons Marc and Brian who believed in me and expressed their faith in my storytelling abilities.

To Tiffany (Binks) who said, "That's exciting!!!" every time I shared with her each journey along the road to completion.

To Neal Siegel who continued to provide me with positive feedback during those luncheons and phone calls when I would convey the next steps I needed to take.

To Princess Parker Rosado who agreed to not only read the early manuscript but offered valuable insight associated with the Latin culture. I am thankful for her helping me get it right.

To Lisa Major who said "Yes" right away when I asked her to read the early manuscript. Her feedback was extremely encouraging all along the way.

To Jeff Kersten for reading the manuscript and offering important insight to the characters as well as the scenes and setting in the manuscript.

To Rob Richardson who went back and re-read "Payback" so he could give me the benefit of his best thinking.